TE

Tempest in a Teacup

Written by Doc White

Edited by Barbara Rabinowitz

Tempest in a Teacup is a work of fiction. Names, characters, places and incidents are either the product of the author's imagination or are used fictitiously, and any resemblance to actual persons, living or dead, business establishments, events or locales is entirely coincidental.

ISBN 978-1482344745

Printed in the United States of America

Acknowledgements

I want to thank my wife, Ceci, for her encouragement; my editor, Barbara Rabinowitz, for her enthusiastic wordsmithing; and my friends, Robert Young Pelton and Al Breitenbach, for their advice and technical expertise.

I turned to many others as I made the long journey from concept to publication: Mike and Kathy Gann, Scott and Suzie Launey, Sandy and Kathy Purdon, Pete Lawrence, John Edwards, Mike Luque, Jim Beckett and all those who put up with my disjointed musings over coffee at the San Diego Yacht Club.

Writing about Vietnam and my time on Swift Boats brought back sharp, sometimes painful memories. But my most poignant and precious reflections dwell on the friendships forged in war and kept strong over half a century.

As a country, we deserted the people of South Vietnam and even turned our backs on our own soldiers, but these soldiers found strength and a sense of belonging from each other and from continuing to support Vietnamese families. I am proud to know such veterans and to have served with them.

Kunming
Irrawaddy
Mandalay
BURMA
Hanoi
Haiphong
LAOS
Gulf of Tonkin
Chiang Mai
Vientiane
Vinh
CHAÎNE ANNAMITIQUE
Mekong
Rangoon
Hue
THAILAND
Nakhon Ratchasima
Mawlamyine
Dawei
Bangkok
ANDAMAN ISLANDS (INDIA)
CAMBODIA
Nha Trang
Phnom Penh
Andaman Sea
Ho Chi Minh City
Gulf of Thailand
Long Xuyen
NICOBAR ISLANDS (INDIA)
Phuket
Songkhla
George Town
Ipoh
MALAYSIA
Strait of Malacca
Medan
Kuala Lumpur
Melaka

Chapter One

The shadows of the jungle night were so dark I could barely make out my crew on the stern of our 50-foot aluminum Swift Boat, powered by its two loud 500-hp GMC engines, now mercifully silent as we lay in wait. There were seven of us, all hot and sweaty and hoping we'd live long enough to never see another jungle. Our faces and hands were darkened and the contour lines of the boat had been carefully concealed by vegetation growing along the riverbank where we'd tied up to an overhanging branch at the muddy water's edge.

Eight months in Vietnam patrolling the Mekong Delta in 1968 had taught us well the lessons of jungle warfare. Break up contour lines. Darken faces, hands, weapons. Even our wristwatches were covered since florescence could be visible for a hundred meters on clear nights. Sounds could be just as unforgiving, even in the noisy jungle during the monsoons. No sound in nature had the metallic sound of weaponry. Of necessity, all the senses were engaged all the time. Even smells foretold of ambushes – theirs with the pungent fish sauce, nuoc mam, which the Vietnamese favored, and ours from the American fondness for red meat, though that was scarce here.

The smell of this ambush was neither meat nor fish but oppressive foreboding. We had intelligence from a Chieu Hoi, a former North Vietnamese soldier who had defected, that a 14-

man NVA anti-boat squad was headed our way. Our job was to deploy ambush teams against a regular North Vietnamese Army team, which was a chilling prospect.

The Viet Cong skirmishes, while dangerous, were unprofessional by military standards. The .50-caliber fire from our boat's twin forward machine guns was intimidating and would often demolish a VC ambush attempt. Trained soldiers wouldn't be so easily discouraged. They would know that the mud bunkers along the riverbanks offered them more protection than the 3/16-inch aluminum hull provided us. And they would be more calculatingly patient before opening fire, waiting until our boats entered the kill zone of their shoulder-launched B-40 rockets.

The consequences of this stepped-up warfare would be devastating on the Swift Boat crews, who already had an unenviable Purple Heart rate of 70% along the lower Mekong Delta. The many wounded were saved by medevac Hueys, keeping the fatality rate mercifully low for a front-line unit. More NVA would most certainly add to the wounded and dying and make extraction even more difficult.

I tried not to think about this as I watched my crew lie in wait onboard boat PCF-45. They made a good team and I was very proud of their abilities. Being prepared and being patient were critical to an ambush. Staring into the darkness, we searched for the very things we tried to prevent the enemy from seeing -- movement, form, reflection -- using "side vision" that helped us recognize objects from an angle at night when they couldn't be detected head-on. The longer the waiting, the harder it was to maintain the high level of vigil, and at 0300 when the body's circadian rhythms flagged, pure adrenalin was what kept us alert, kept us alive.

Lifting the band covering my watch, I confirmed that it was now 0315 – time for our radio check. Using the handset on the PRC-45 radio, I initiated three microphone clicks and received two in return from our sister Swift Boat. The immediate reply indicated that Ross, the skipper of PCF-73, was alert and aware that we were entering the time of night when the VC deployments would be reaching their destinations with time to spare before sunrise. Covering any distance in the Mekong Delta required boats. Our ambush was set up at the junction of the Dam Doi River and two canals we'd named Tom and Jerry. It was here we thought we had the best chance of intercepting troops from the north. We sat back at a distance in the dense riverbank foliage.

I slipped aft to check the crew and ensure our readiness. The deck felt cool and damp to my bare feet. Riggs, Charley and Brooks were all alert. They were ambush veterans and they knew that a job well done tonight would make the daytime patrols somewhat less dangerous. It was how we measured success.

It was 0405 when I heard the sound of a paddle scrapping the side of a canoe and almost immediately saw the dark shape exiting the Tom Canal and moving into the Dam Doi River, making a left turn to parallel our position. I slipped the safety off my Swedish K and reached up to tap the foot of Zeke, my gunner's mate in the Twin-50 tub just above the pilothouse. As planned, he would initiate the ambush by firing a pop-flare behind our positions. The sound of the flare would spark the ambush, and the flare itself, with its million-candlepower white phosphorous flame, would illuminate the sampans.

Now, with a fist, I pounded twice on Zeke's foot. Almost immediately, I heard the pop of the fired flare joined by the rapid staccato of M2, M60 and M16 fire. The tracers, loaded every third round, appeared as an almost continuous red-to-orange line. Night became day and dark shapes came out of the shadows and appeared frozen in the harsh light of the flare. What was left of the sampan appeared to no longer be a threat; it no longer appeared to be much of anything.

I called for a cease-fire and started the engines to take a closer look. Boyd, the bow gunner, untied us from the tree and we got underway to check the canoe with our sister boat also proceeding upstream to cover us.

The Browning M2 machine gun, with its half-inch rounds, had been designed for aircraft and tank guns during World War II. A fearful weapon, the M2 had proven itself extremely effective against lightly armored enemy aircraft and ships. At 75 meters, against a wooden canoe and the five onboard, it had shown no mercy. Despite its waterlogged condition, the sampan was burning and uniforms on the dying VC were smoldering.

With a grapple, we pulled the canoe alongside to collect the bodies, weapons and anything else that might be of intelligence value. It was clear that these were local VC. Although they were carrying SKSs, AK47s and a B40, they were not NVA.

We secured the bodies and weapons on the fantail and sunk the canoe with as much speed as possible. I was anxious to get downriver fast. It was already 0445 and the sun would be up in an hour. We were deep in enemy territory and would become more vulnerable in daylight. By dawn, we needed to be on a wider river, the Song Cau Lon, near *Sea Float*, our home.

Home? Hell, what we called home was a series of barges tied up in the middle of the widest part of the Cau Lon River, which flowed into both the Gulf of Thailand and the South China Sea. Home for us was a rewards destination for helo pilots who earned two points toward an air medal every time they landed – not that we begrudged them their due for braving the dangers and medevacing the wounded. What made our home unique was not so much its location but its inhabitants -- a strange family of specials ops warriors: SEALs, Underwater Demolition Teams, Swift Boats crews, Green Berets and the Montagnards from the Vietnam highlands who worked with them, Kit Carson Scouts, Nung Chinese and their CIA handlers, plus an assortment of pet pythons, monkeys, dogs and birds.

Fortunately, the tidal flow under our barge home produced a current of some 10-plus knots that proved good insurance against waterborne sappers and any harm they might bring – like trying to blow us to kingdom come. We never wondered why the USO shows bypassed our little piece of the world.

What we lacked in government-sponsored morale boosting, we got from our cooks who whipped up some truly creative and great tasting meals, winning the hearts and minds of some of the most dangerous men in the world of war. The smell of fresh-baked bread rendered the steeliest warrior strangely boyish and nostalgic for home. There was no warm bread or warm grub of any kind out on patrol. What we had were C-Rations (officially replaced in 1958 by the more delectable-sounding MCIs for Meal, Combat, Individual). But we still called them C-Rations and worse. These meals were only halfway palatable when served hot with lots of Tabasco, but there was no way to heat meals on the boat, though some of us learned that C-4 worked nicely as sterno.

While on patrol, our generators were inoperative and no one was allowed inside the cabin. When my hankering for warm beanie-weenies got the best of me one day on routine patrol, I thought I'd heat my can on the engines.

Taking out my P-38 can opener, which had been the U.S. warrior's most important all-purpose tool since WWII, I opened my beanie-weenie combo, pulled up the starboard-engine hatch and placed my meal right on top. Brilliant, I thought to myself just before we came under heavy fire.

Once clear of the kill zone, I ordered both boats to beach right and mortar, which meant driving the bow into the riverbank, holding the boat there with forward throttle and mortaring the jungle for 10 minutes. When fire was no longer returned, we checked out the ambush site and recovered a B-40 rocket-launching tube with wire initiators. We found some blood but no bodies. Our own damage assessment revealed no casualties but our boat had been blasted by my unattended can simmering on the engine and we had suffered extensive beanie-weenie shrapnel damage. Long after I'd scraped off the last bean and the engine man, Diesel, had forgiven me, there lingered a faint smell of beanie weenies that had died in vain.

Right now, home aboard *Sea Float* meant more than some decent grub; it meant a respite from patrol, from constant high alert. The 73-boat took the lead and we started back with our weapons reloaded, safeties off. The fastest that the slowest boat would go was our speed. Thirty knots was our top speed. It never seemed fast enough.

Looking back, I should have anticipated what happened next. As we approached the last half mile before leaving the narrow Dam Doi River to enter the Cau Lon River, there was an "S" turn -- a full 90 degrees to the left, then 90 to the right. As we finished the first turn and steadied up, they struck. Opening fire with B40s and small arms, they had waited until the 73-boat was right on top of them, ensuring that the twin 50s in the upper turret could not be unleashed on the ambush site. The B40 hit the bow, exploding on the forward gunner and helmsman. The boat continued directly into the riverbank with its engines still in full throttle. We had been just starting our left turn when the ambush began, putting the 73-boat between the ambush site and us and making it impossible for us to open fire. The gun crew on the 73-boat fantail was firing point blank at the enemy troops dug in on the riverbank some 15 meters away.

Jonesy, the aft-gunner on the 73-boat, picked up an enemy-thrown grenade and tossed it back in the NVA bunker. The explosion reduced the fire on us, but increased the fire on the fantail of the 73. Jonesy went down and all fire from his boat ceased. The enemy could now concentrate totally on us.

One amazing thing about combat is that time takes on a new dimension. Somehow amid the deafening, disorienting barrage of a firefight with its relentless deadly chaos, everything slows down. Things come into sharper focus. Emotions become clinical observations of fact. Any pre-action nerves I might have harbored always evaporated in the knowledge that I was as prepared as I was ever going to be for the unexpected and the unthinkable.

Our only chance was to get a tow line on the 73-boat and drag her clear of the ambush. We came alongside, keeping our sister boat between the enemy position and us. This shielded us, but didn't stop the rounds that easily pierced the thin aluminum hull of the 73. My intention was to give the forward gunner our tow line, but he was down -- his body crumpled, his helmet on deck some 10 feet away, still strapped to his head. There was no sign of Ross, the skipper, and the helmsman was unconscious or dead. I needed to attach the line to the forward bollard and secure the engines. Quickly but carefully, I stepped across, threw the eye splice over the forward bollard, ran aft to the pilothouse to secure the throttles, then slipped and fell, banging my head on the helm. Even with my helmet, the fall nearly knocked me unconscious. Using my hands to regain my footing, I slipped again and realized that I was sliding on blood.

I yanked the throttles back into reverse to clear the vessel from the riverbank. The screws caught, but the boat had wedged itself into the bank and was not going to immediately break free. Just outside the port hatch of the pilothouse I could see into part of a slit trench that the NVA had dug. From deep down I saw an NVA solider, a woman, sighting an M3 American grease gun. God, what an antique! I was still pondering the effectiveness of the M3 relic when I watched her fire on me. I felt the first .45 hit me just above the sternum in my flak jacket, knocking me back against the bulkhead. The firing continued, but I couldn't respond. The sound receded as blackness gathered.

In the grayness of my brain, there was pain -- not anywhere, but everywhere, then total darkness. The next time I was aware of anything, there was less gray but the pain had not diminished and was concentrated in my chest and head. After a while I realized that I was coming around.

I was face-down in the mud, my arms behind me. I could see very little and there was now no pain, only numbness. I thought that I might be dead or so close that it was only semantics. I felt tired, completely used up. I had not had a full night's sleep in eight months. I should just let go I thought. I needed to rest.

The next time I came to, things were more sharply focused, even in the dark. I saw a campfire and realized I wasn't going to get any rest, not now and probably never, except in death. I was sitting, bound to a tree, arms tied behind me just above the elbows and my legs were spread eagle and staked to the ground. A squad of NVA stood around a small campfire where rice was cooking. To one side of the fire, I saw two of my crew, Riggs and Charley, both with frightening, absurdly happy grins. It took me awhile to realize that it wasn't Riggs and Charley as I had known them but only parts of them. Their fate now awaited me.

After the NVA finished their meal, they turned their attention to me. The young lady who had shot me walked over and squatted between my legs, facing me, her head level with mine. Her English was flawless, and in an almost monotonous voice, she described what she was going to do to me. Using her knife, she cut off the remnants of my bush jacket. As she promised, she then started making cuts on my chest. The knife was so sharp I almost didn't feel the cuts. She took her time and my mind took itself to a faraway place where this couldn’t be happening. With every cut, I retreated further and further inside myself. I don't think I fully comprehended the situation until she went behind my back and returned with a piece of my little finger dangling from her hand.

Chapter Two

At first I thought it was my own screaming that had awakened me but it was my phone that saved me from my recurring nightmare. I answered it half-mad, half-relieved that someone dared enter my world, my little island hidden among North Carolina's Outer Banks.

"Beau? That you?"

"Yes...Is that you?"

"That it is, my brother – the one and only, your savior, saving your ass one more time from a life without me. That is if FedEx can find your island in the back country. I'm sending you a plane ticket to come see me in San Diego. I want you on that plane tomorrow. Beau, I need you.

"I don't know. I don't know..."

"Beau, I'm sorry about Helen."

"Thanks..."

"Beau, I seriously need you on a mission and, frankly, I think you need to get away – at least for a while. In other words, get your butt on that flight or I will personally come get you. Pack light. I've got everything you need. See you tomorrow. Out for now."

Replacing the receiver, I checked my watch. It was 3:45 a.m. my time. Hell, it was late for the Californian too. Damn! Sleep came so rarely these days, and when it did, there were the dreams. No point in going back to bed.

As I went about washing my face and brushing my teeth, I studied myself in the mirror. I had aged in the months since Helen's death. My six-foot-two frame was lanky, but normally carried 210 pounds. While I hadn't bothered to weigh myself, I doubted I topped 170. My face was gaunt and my eyes, normally green, were so dull they didn't appear to have a color. What they did have was *The Look*, that "1,000-yard stare," seen all too often in combat. My hair, once light brown, was graying at an accelerated rate. The year-round tan was gone, replaced by a pallor that was probably the major cause of concern for my friends and neighbors. I looked like I was dying. Helen would be pissed.

I went to the kitchen and ground some beans for coffee. There was a light frost outside, so I lit a fire in the small fireplace in the kitchen.

Helen and I had designed and built the fireplace in the kitchen, just as we had done the entire cottage except for a few projects we had subbed to local carpenters and an occasional specialist from Raleigh. We had started with the remnants of a small hunting shack on an island just inside the Outer Banks. This unnamed island was uninhabited and unreachable except by a causeway that crossed a pristine marsh of sinewy lush grasses and cypress trees. Helen had fallen in love with the Outer Banks, where I was raised, and she had put all this love into our island, our Eden. After we planted an orchard and garden, we left the rest of the island alone to thrive in the glory of its own natural habitat. Power was supplied by solar panels, wind generators and a back-up diesel generator. A deepwater creek allowed us a dock and gave us access to Pamlico Sound and the Atlantic Ocean.

Our lives revolved through the seasons and the rhythms of our own passionate sharing of a time and space so precious and so complete that we seemed to need nothing else.

Helen loved to paint in her small studio built over the boat dock. Her oil and watercolor work, depicting the Outer Banks, was well received by art critics and collectors alike and we met with her New York agent twice a year.

We never tired of exploring our island and those up and down the coast. Helen was especially thrilled when she sighted the native wild horses flashing along the sand dunes. They were often the subject of her paintings and my photography. We found ourselves collaborating on a book depicting all the beauty of the Outer Banks. It seemed only right that we had wound up living on an island since we met on another island in another ocean.

Our first encounter took place off the coast of Southern California on a diving trip to Catalina Island. I was still in the Navy and she was working on her degree in art history at UC San Diego. Our shared loved of diving and fascination with wildlife overcame her initial dislike of my being a naval officer. She hated the Vietnam War. It had taken her younger brother his first year as a second lieutenant in the Marine Corps. She railed against the war's great human cost, its global ramifications and political deception. But she kept an open mind when it came to me and that was what mattered.

After dating eight months, I took Helen home to North Carolina. It was her first visit to the South and was nothing like she expected. The people she met were educated, well-traveled and interesting. Though she never admitted it, I think Helen half-expected to be met at the airport by the Ku Klux Klan and taken on an excursion by characters straight out of *Deliverance.* She was pleasantly surprised with my mother's gracious home in Raleigh, but when she first saw the Outer Banks, she fell in love. To this day, I believe it was this love that helped me win her heart forever. We were married a week after I got out of the Navy and came home to live in North Carolina.

We found our island, built our house and bought a boat, the *Blue Crab,* a 24-foot walk-around outboard with a small cabin. The 250-hp Yamaha engine made it possible for us to visit the islands and the small fishing towns up and down the coast. We'd collect bay scallops and oysters, dive some of the wrecks along the "Graveyard of the Atlantic" off Cape Hatteras and photograph the swamp bears sighted in the early dawn hours along the Pungo Canal. Our dearly loved and sorely missed black Labrador Sadie liked to bark at the bottlenose dolphins that rode our bow wake up this inland waterway, and I was certain that the dolphins squealed back at Sadie. They were clearly communicating on a level too advanced for humans.

Helen reveled in my stories of growing up in towns like Nags Head, Kill Devil Hills and Ocracoke accompanied by tales of the "high tiders" or “hoi toiders” who live along the eastern coast, especially in Carteret County. She liked the dialects that transformed words like seagulls and oysters into “seagirls” and “erysters." Believing that English may have been our second language, Helen came to know and cherish the words that made up the fabric of the locals’ lives and myths.

When “seagirls” became a nuisance dropping their “eryster” shells on the two-lane blacktop as a way to get them open and leaving the razor-sharp remnants as unexpected hazards for motorists, the community found a quick remedy for the rash of flat tires. The solution: no task force, no blue-ribbon committee, just a decision to paint white “seagirls” on the highway. No self-respecting, greedy “seagirl” would drop an “eryster” where it thought another “seagirl” could get it. And so the folklore grew itself another story.

Helen particularly loved Ocracoke Island, one of the most remote of the Outer Banks’ barrier chain and the place where Blackbeard supposedly lived. Like all the Outer Banks, Ocracoke’s landscape consisted of windswept sand dunes and salt marshes with a harbor entrance that constantly changed with the tides and storms. For years, in the early 1900s, along the treacherous banks, ship captains had whistled for a mysterious dolphin to lead them through the maze of shifting sandbars into port. There were times, when the wind was just right, that I thought I could still hear those ancient captains.

Helen immersed herself in all the folklore and the panoply of nature's own wondrous storytelling. Her eye for color, texture and movement gave her paintings a life of their own. When she moved from oils to watercolors, her work became mystical. Helen's skill at making reality ethereal dramatically improved my photography, helping me see more of what was right in front of me. But since her death, I had closed off the world and shut down my receptive senses. I hadn't taken a single photograph or even looked at my old work. My editor's initial condolences had turned into worrisome demands to fulfill previous commitments; but I had not responded, feeling incapable of ever taking another photograph – that is until Magic's wake-up call.

Standing in the middle of the kitchen, I was struck by all the neglect that met my gaze. Nothing had been touched since Helen's death – the house, the garden, the *Blue Crab*. I had let everything go and it showed. I was disgusted with myself because I knew Helen would be sick at heart with the sad state of our little paradise.

I slumped down in the chair and finished my coffee as I remembered how our idyllic world had been so shattered. The tumor was just the first sign of a relentless cancer that seemed undaunted by months of chemo, radiation, convalescence and continuous attempts at new treatments. Hope and resolve turned into disappointment, fear, exhaustion and, finally, resignation – the dark cascading spiral of cancer. I'd never felt so helpless and I'd gone up against some badass enemies, but this was beyond all my training and know-how. I tried to stay busy, tried to gain some control over the things I could fix and made damn sure I was there for Helen with whatever she needed that I could provide. But in the end, what she needed was a cure that never came. She died in our home surrounded by her loved ones, her art and her island. And one day, I awoke to an empty bed and I couldn't find one good reason to get up. Nothing seemed to matter. Friends stopped by to check on me and I noticed that they often performed the simple chores I neglected. I think there was always some surprise when I opened the door because I often didn't bother. And I must have looked a sight. I even scared myself some mornings, so I just quit looking in the mirror. The visits declined and the days came and went without much notice -- until now with this damn call from Magic.

I don't think I consciously decided to go. Too apathetic to make a real decision, I simply followed Magic's orders. I found myself closing the house and packing. I made a phone call to my closest neighbor and longtime friend, Ned Wood, asking him to watch over the property. At first, he didn't recognize my voice but his surprise at hearing from me turned into heartfelt well wishes for a good trip. He was happy to help and happier still to have use of the *Blue Crab*.

Within an extraordinarily busy 24 hours of my usual do-nothing life, I was on my way -- moving forward without a plan -- but moving forward.

Ned delivered me to the small airport in Moorhead City, where a commuter plane took me to Raleigh/Durham to board an American Airlines flight to San Diego. And the seemingly immovable object that was me was airborne.

Chapter Three

There were more people on the small commuter plane than I had seen in the entire past year. It was a new millennium and its beginning had come and gone without much notice from me. I felt suddenly overwhelmed. This was a mistake. I felt totally out of place. Small spaces were always difficult for me and now I had to get my six-two frame into one of these ridiculous seats. When the prop engines started, I recalled how I'd flown on much more deafening air transport in much worse shape with bullets flying. It was then I realized I could handle this – no sweat.

It was my nightmares from those other places, from another time that seemed insurmountable. And these memories never seemed to dim. They were just as vivid and just as frightening as they'd been years before when they were fresh.

The moment after the North Vietnamese soldier displayed my severed finger, her grin suddenly disappeared and she looked strangely broken. There was no other way to describe it. I'd seen a lot of things in battle but I never found any of them easy to put into words.

Running the rivers, our battles consisted of close-quarter firefights with machine guns and rifles. We saw firsthand the devastating impact of modern weapons on the human body. People instinctively fight tenaciously for their lives and sometimes survive savage wounds. What we saw wasn't cleaned up for the viewing audience – bodies torn apart with bones broken and organs exposed – everything covered in mud and blood until it was almost unrecognizable as human. Accompanying the carnage was the soundtrack of screams, frantic radio calls for medevacs and orders yelled over gunfire and explosions. What wasn't hard to comprehend, even for a FNG (Fucking New Guy), was the moment a person went from alive to limp, lifeless ragdoll -- when all the lights went out.

This was just what was happening in front of me – the soldier torturing me was gone. Her eyes went blank and she crumpled in a contorted heap. In that split second, the jungle erupted with the noise of small arms and grenades. Caught completely unaware, the North Vietnamese platoon fell apart.

No sooner had it started than it was over – that disturbing after-action quiet with its ever-present smell of cordite and the low moaning of the wounded and dying, whose ranks I had joined.

But I wasn't dead yet, though I was surely hallucinating. There, in front of me, was the smiling face of an Asian black man in black pajamas cutting me loose and helping me up. His first words of introduction were "SEALs Never Forget."

This was my formal introduction to James Louis Black, nickname and call sign "Magic." He saved my life and became my best friend. But we had met earlier during my third month in country, when his SEAL team had been caught in a surprise firefight. Heavy monsoon overcast prevented helo support, so the call came to the Swift Boats. I was in the lead boat as we left the main river, entering a narrow canal with barely a foot of clearance on either side of the boat and open ground all around. The term "sitting ducks" came to mind, but I shook it off as I tossed out a snake trying to hitch a ride.

As we moved farther and farther along the canal, I could see tracer fire up ahead. Under our covering fire, the SEALs piled onboard. All were wounded, some seriously. Unable to turn around, I took control from the aft helm, and under withering fire, backed down the constricted canal. It seemed to take forever to reach the river where we had room to run full-bore. We were in a race back to the base to get help for the wounded. Since that incident, the SEAL teams had adopted my crew and they came to my rescue while I still had most of my fingers and toes.

James Louis Black came from San Francisco, the beloved offspring of a black mother and Chinese father, both professors at UC Berkeley. An only child, Magic was given all the gifts of his rich heritage. He was fluent in several Chinese dialects and studied art history and Shaolin Kempo Karate.

At six feet, 240 pounds, Magic was powerfully built. His brown skin was a perfect setting for his bright oriental eyes that always appeared amused at his unfolding life. He constantly reminded me of the first line from

Rafael Sabatini's book, *Scaramouche*: "He was born with the gift of laughter, and a sense that the world was mad."

Though exposed to prejudice as both an African and Chinese American, Magic had the rare good fortune to be born in the right place at the right time to the right parents and then to come of age just when his particular mix of intelligence and skills was most needed. He received an appointment to the U.S. Naval Academy and later joined the SEALs. It seemed only fitting that Magic joined an organization with the unique capability to operate on sea, air and land and even underwater.

Though the need for a program like the SEALs was recognized in World War II, when the U.S. Navy realized the importance of having a special force to reconnoiter landing beaches, it was President Kennedy, with his understanding of the situation in Southeast Asia, who saw the need for unconventional warfare carried out by special operations. In his 1961 speech about putting a man on the Moon, Kennedy also announced $100 million for special operations for guerilla and counter-guerilla units, which meant funding for SEALs. They got their training at two Naval Amphibious Bases: the Little Creek Naval Base near Virginia Beach and Coronado in San Diego. From Coronado, Magic went on to serve 24 years in the Navy, rising in rank to admiral. He worked in special operations, black ops and anti-terrorism.

Most of what he did "never happened" and he certainly "was never there."

Helen had loved Magic, though at first she couldn't reconcile her image of a combat veteran with the well-read, caring and gentle man she came to know. It took her awhile to understand that she could hate the war and embrace the warrior, even the professional soldier. She realized quicker than most that it was the politicians who sent young soldiers, many who were drafted, to suffer, die and take the fall for Washington's deceptions, blunders and failed policy in Vietnam. Her brother was just one of the 58,000 who never came back. She knew he would want her to be welcoming to those who did.

After retiring from the Navy, Magic settled in San Diego, where he continued his studies in Chinese art. He moved aboard his beloved ketch-rigged *Freedom*, which he spent two years restoring and later sailing to points south.

I had not seen Magic during this time. I did follow his exploits through his letters and postcards from exotic ports of call. Ours was a friendship, like many forged in extreme circumstances, that endured with no regard for time or space. It was always there, something to count on and renew, without missing a beat, over a couple of beers.

With the announcement of our final approach into San Diego's Lindbergh Field, I realized that this was the first block of time I'd spent thinking about something other than death and loss. I was stunned by my own sense of betrayal to Helen's memory.

From the port side of the plane, I could make out the Naval Amphibious Base on Coronado's Silver Strand, home of the Navy SEALs and Special Boat Operations where we had trained in Swift Boats. Two aircraft carriers were lined up against the dock at North Island Naval Air Station. As my plane finally touched down, its engines roared into reverse on what I remembered as a short, unforgiving runway. The terminal was another matter. It had grown considerably larger and busier in the past 20 years but it still obviously served a Navy town and many Chargers and Padres fans. Here was a whole other world outside my island, my self-imposed isolation. I wasn’t sure I was ready for all this but I was here.

Chapter Four

As I sat back in the cab from the airport, it was incredibly obvious to me how much San Diego had changed. No longer a sleepy Navy town, it was now the eighth largest city in the U.S. and the second largest in California. The 10-minute ride through downtown and out to Shelter Island to the address Magic had provided, 1011 Anchorage Lane, gave me a brief, but eye-opening tour of all San Diego had to offer. Word had definitely gotten out about the city's weather, natural beauty and dynamic ability to reinvent itself.

I knew that Shelter Island, a man-made peninsula, was home to marinas, hotels, restaurants and the famous San Diego Yacht Club, which turned out to be Magic's address. The guard at the gate checked for my name and gave me directions to D dock, slip 26. I was told to look for the *Empress*, a jade-colored trawler.

Grabbing my duffel, I followed the guard's directions to a beautiful 65-foot green fishing trawler. An older wooden vessel, the *Empress* had spent her years in loving hands. The paint was flawless; the bright work sparkled. She would make a fine vessel for cruising the Pacific coast from Alaska to Cape Horn. I took a moment to admire the fine design and the hours of care that had gone into the *Empress*.

When I called out for permission to come aboard, Magic's booming voice preceded his appearance at the open cabin door.

“My good friend, welcome!"

“Lieutenant Beauregard MacEvoy reporting for duty.”

As I saluted, Magic’s grin widened. Seeing his face brought back a rush of emotions, a collage of all the times we’d shared, enjoyed and amazingly lived through. He looked thinner than I remembered but I was sure he was thinking the same thing about me.

The first time I saw that unforgettable Magic smile was when he saved my ass in the jungle. There would be more close calls and innumerable rounds of beer. He was best man at my wedding and our first invited guest to the island. Now I was seeing Magic for the first time since Helen’s death.

As I hugged my friend, something inside me just let go. I had no control over my emotions. Tears filled my eyes and sobs replaced breathing. My knees started to buckle. I was losing it. Magic held me up, something he had done before. He took me into the main salon and put me on the couch. He didn’t say a word and didn’t leave my side except to get me some water, which I nearly choked on. Pulling myself together seemed not to be an option. I couldn’t stop crying. I felt as if my heart was being sucked from my chest.

With his arms around me, Magic let me know that I was in a safe place to suddenly become a blubbering idiot. “I’m sorry I wasn’t there for you when Helen died but I’m here now, not somewhere on the high seas. We think we understand the fragility of life because we've seen combat. But we don't -- not really. We forget that one minute you're fine and the next minute you're fucked, even if no one is shooting at you. We get into our routines of life and we take so much for granted. I know you didn't take Helen for granted, but I'm sure you believed you'd grow old together. You hurt so much because you had so much and no one will ever be able to say they know how you feel. We spent many a night talking about this in the jungle. We lost good friends, friendships forged under heavy fire and in the life-sucking swamps of the Mekong Delta.

Without letting go of me, Magic reached up to a shelf and pulled down a bottle of Scotch and two glasses. He poured healthy shots as he carefully chose his words. "I know you're still trying to figure out how you could have saved Helen, but you did all you could. You're the most courageous warrior I have ever known. The SEALs, hugging your boat deck when you came up the canal to save us, remember you standing at the helm with rounds hitting your flak jacket so fast that it danced. I couldn't believe they only retrieved 12 rounds from your jacket. Seemed like hundreds. Jesus, you earned the Navy Cross."

Magic lifted his glass and I followed suit. "To Helen," he toasted and I echoed his sentiment as our glasses clinked.

I was emotionally and physically drained as I sprawled on the couch and put my head on a pillow. From his end of the sofa, Magic turned to face me.

"Whatever doubts you may have about your current abilities, you can just forget them. Death makes us doubt everything. But I know your talents and I need you almost as badly as I think you need this mission."

Though I listened intently to everything Magic was telling me, I couldn't seem to respond. I was dead tired, as if I'd been going for a long time without sleep or food or even human contact because in truth I had.

Magic stood and looked straight through me. "When was the last time you ate, Beau? You look like a refugee. It's a good thing I'm here to get your white ass back in shape."

I'm not sure how much longer Magic kept talking because I just crashed. What finally awakened me was the smell of stew -- unmistakably Magic's famous cioppino. Adding one last dash of Tabasco, he turned to me with a triumphant look.

"If this doesn't bring you back to the living, nothing will."

"Well, you sure saved us in Nam with the Tabasco Family's *Charlie Ration Cookbook* – almost made our C-Rations tasty or maybe it was just all we could taste was the hot sauce."

As Magic set the table, I took my first good look around. The interior of the vessel was as beautiful as the exterior – all varnished teak and mahogany. The salon opened to the galley.

Lighting was provided by antique brass hurricane lamps, old, but polished to a mirror finish.

Slipping back into the galley, Magic leaned over a gimbaled gas oven, opened the door and brought out freshly baked French bread. He then ladled his thick stew into a huge pewter tureen. Without looking, he yelled over his shoulder for me to pour some of the Montrachet open on the table.

Though I felt positively drugged by the powerful smells filling the cabin, I managed to locate two glasses and pour the wine. Magic had awakened a ravenous monster. I ate until I hurt and was upset that I couldn't get down more than two bowls of cioppino and half a baguette. When I finally took a breath and looked up, I met Magic's grin. "This has to be the first decent homemade meal you've eaten since Helen died. Am I right?"

I nodded wiping my chin and settling back in my chair. "Now that you've invited me here, allowed me to fall apart and mended me with a feast and fine wine, I'm still not sure what you have in mind."

"I need your help and I think you need to be out in this world eating and drinking and enjoying my scintillating company. There's more wine to go with the story I'm about to tell you. It starts and ends with the teacup you found."

Chapter Five

During my last month in Vietnam, I was stationed at our base in An Thoi where our mother ship, the *Beaufort,* was anchored on the southern tip of Phu Quoc Island, Vietnam's largest island, located in the Gulf of Thailand.

My assignment was to train new crews for their patrols and to let them know which American rock 'n' roll the enemy seemed to like best, meaning they shot at us less -- the unofficial soundtrack for our psyops. If the VC weren't ever going to make peace with us, perhaps they'd succumb to our music. My personal favorite was CCR's *Rolling on the River*.

Since it wasn't particularly arduous duty, I had some time to spend diving the small islands and coral reefs around Phu Quoc. Hon Tay Island, near Hon Da Ban Reef, was especially intriguing. Hon Tay's coral reef, or bommie as the Australian Aborigines named such places, rose to within 12 feet of the surface and sprawled out in glorious colors across 100 feet before dropping off to a level sand bridge to the main island on one side and straight down to 19 fathoms on the other.

On previous dives, I had worked the 100-foot shelf coming off the coral walls spending the last full measure of my air at the top of the bommie, enjoying the anemones, clown fish, small crabs and all the things that seemed to come to life purely for my enjoyment.

I once again noticed what had caught my eye before – one place where the world below revealed glimpses of regular angles. It had been my experience in diving and in jungle warfare that straight lines and right angles were almost always man-made. With about 200 pounds of air left in my tank, I started working to free the angular object from the coral, though everything seemed to have fused together eons ago. Finally, I chiseled out a lump of something and took it to the surface for closer examination.

I showed my find to Jack, the boatswain mate, who was recovering from a minor wound and had asked to come with me. He had been tending our small boat and snorkeling above the reef. His initial response was not encouraging.

"Jesus, Lieutenant! No disrespect, but this is undoubtedly the shittiest piece of coral down there!"

Jack was definitely not seeing what I thought I saw and I didn't enlighten him. Back onboard the *Beaufort,* I went to work on my find with muriatic acid and metal picks, liberated from the ship's dentist. By dabbing the acid on the coral, I was slowly able to reduce the one-foot chunk of coral. Whatever was embedded in the coral's clutches was white porcelain or ivory. Bronze elements were also revealed, but I concentrated on the sections of white until I exposed an exquisite porcelain cup, small, only two inches in diameter with an intricate blue oriental design. Remarkably, it was perfectly whole and stunning, a real treasure.

Turning my attention to the bronze section, I found it even more secretive than the teacup and in much worse shape. I finally retrieved a bronze trigger guard connected to what was left of two or three gun barrels with only about four inches of metal remaining. It seemed like the metal was decaying before my eyes, so I dropped the whole thing in varnish to preclude its further demise. The entire procedure had taken all my spare time for over a week. Now I had only three more days and one very early wake-up call and I'd be on my way home.

The next day the guys, who weren't on patrol, threw me a going-away party at the O Club – a Quonset hut that looked like and probably was a relic from WWII. We had a full house. Magic had finagled himself a helo ride to join the party. He added his own stories to those already circulating about my shadier exploits.

It was late when the rowdy warriors stumbled out of the O Club. With too much San Miguel and Bau Mui Bau beer and a mysterious punch with questionable origins, the revelers returned to the *Beaufort* to find their bunks. Magic and I remained on deck awhile, admiring a clear, star-festooned sky.

I told Magic about my find as we shared our last drink in Vietnam. From my description, he thought the cup was probably Chinese, not a Japanese sake cup, as the size suggested. He asked to see it and I promised to bring it round after breakfast.

At 0400, the skipper unexpectedly awakened me. There was an unscheduled flight in 30 minutes, and if I could get there, I could leave two days early. I hurriedly dressed, gathered my few things and threw them in a bag. I left Magic the cup, pistol and a note saying I would see him in the "world."

Over the years, we often talked about the "treasure." Magic continued to research the cup and its guardian pistol as he finished his doctorate in Chinese art history. While reading George MacDonald Fraser's series, Magic found that the antihero, Flashman, described a unique pistol called an "Adams Multi-shot," made in the mid-1850s by the British gun manufacturer, Beaumont Adams. It was very rare.

Magic became convinced that this was the pistol I had found. In its present state, our pistol was worthless but Magic begrudgingly admitted that it had been a stroke of genius to dip it in varnish so we'd have enough to identify. I knew it wasn't so much genius as all I had available, but kept this fact to myself.

The cup proved more elusive in determining its origins, its age or its value. Magic had vowed to be relentless. As he poured me yet another glass of wine, I had a feeling I was about to get a teacup update that would surprise and amaze me.

Chapter Six

Always a good storyteller, Magic set the stage by bringing out a beautiful teak box. He opened the top and showed me the teacup inside. I imagined all the stories it could tell. It was as exquisite as I remembered.

"I can't begin to tally the hours I've put into uncovering the secrets of this damn teacup," Magic confessed. "It started as a quest and is now an obsession. The more I discovered, the more I knew I was searching for something very rare -- eggshell-thin porcelain with colored designs inlaid not overlaid.

"Finally, I came upon some writings about the technique and discovered it is very rare indeed. In fact, there are no surviving examples except your cup. I was right to keep it in a lockbox because it is a treasure.

"When I discussed the cup with a UCLA art history professor, she told me that this particular porcelain technique no longer existed, its artistry somehow lost over the ages. Any surviving porcelain would be priceless. She believed that the style was solely for the use of the Manchus from Manchuria, who came to power in China in the 17th century, founding the Qing Dynasty that lasted until 1911. If she was right, these porcelain treasures and the artists who created them were never allowed to leave the Forbidden City in Beijing.

"When I showed her a picture of the cup, she seemed astonished, peppering me with questions about where it had been found. I gave her something close to the truth, a story about a SEAL sending me a photograph of something he'd found in Vietnam."

I needed to stretch my legs and indicated that we go topside to finish this saga. After the dinner, the wine and the good company, I felt better than I had in a long time. Emerging from the cabin into a balmy Southern California night, I sensed some stirring of life in me that had been dormant much too long. The Magic Man was using all his considerable powers to get me excited about a priceless Chinese teacup found with an ancient British pistol on a Vietnamese reef. I still had no idea what my part would be in all this. It all seemed worlds away from another lifetime, but for now I was content to go along for the ride.

Magic popped into view with two cognacs and a couple of cigars. It was then I knew we were in for some serious storytelling.

After lighting my cigar and then his, Magic effortlessly took us time-traveling to China in the 1800s. "This very isolated nation would accept only silver for her highly valued tea, opening just one port to foreign ships and refusing to allow other countries access to Chinese markets. The mighty British East India Company decided this trade imbalance had to end and invested massively in opium production. The British, joined by the Americans, began selling opium to Chinese smugglers who illegally sold the drug to their countrymen for recreational use. The smugglers paid in silver and the British had a growing source of silver needed to buy tea. With the run on Chinese silver and the growing problem of addiction, the Qing Dynasty tried to end the opium trade but Britain fought back in the first Opium War from 1839 to 1842. China lost the war, had to open new ports to Britain and cede Hong Kong to Queen Victoria. It was not the Brit's finest hour, nor ours."

"And it all came back to bite us in the butt with strung-out soldiers in Vietnam and a huge market for heroin right here in the States," I added, interrupting Magic's history lesson.

"But there's also something to be said for American ingenuity in this dirty business. Because of the incredible fortunes involved in the opium trade, the fastest ships were highly prized, making the Baltimore Clippers the must-have vessels. They didn't just look fast with their sharp V-shaped hull and raked masts and stern, they could clock speeds in excess of 25 knots, outrunning pursuers and getting goods to port in record time. Baltimore Clippers still hold some speed records from America to China.

"It was one of these ships that I think held our teacup and pistol. Poor charts, monsoons, typhoons and pirates took 25% of these ships. One Chinese pirate was supposedly the richest man in the world, worth $50 million.

"I believe that an American clipper, the *Lady Anne*, which was smuggling opium up and down the China coast, held our treasure. The second officer onboard wrote a book and spoke about a porcelain cargo. It also seems he won a very unique pistol from a British officer during a stop in Gibraltar for repairs before continuing the voyage south through the Atlantic and across the Indian Ocean to China. This second officer chronicles the entire trip and talks about finally making it into an isolated harbor north of Hong Kong. In exchange for opium, the ship took on antique vases, china and cases of "gold slippers," small gold bars shaped like Chinese slippers.

"Trying to beat the monsoon season, the *Lady Anne* headed out only to be caught in a terrible storm in the South China Sea and was driven west under bare poles for three days until the main mast broke. This parted the planks, increasing the intake of water for the next two days and making the ship ride lower and lower in the water. When the weather suddenly cleared, the crew spotted land on the horizon and decided it was time to abandon ship. They loaded supplies into long boats and headed for terra firma only to realize that it was the eye of the storm that had passed and that they had the rest of the storm to weather in their small craft. Only one boat rode out the storm and the surviving crew members were held prisoner in the Kingdom of Cambodia. The second officer lived to tell the tale. And you've just survived my retelling of this great story only to be told that it doesn't end here."

Magic finished the last of his cognac and waited for my response but I had no idea where he was going with all this.

"Okay, I'm cautiously curious about what you have in mind for an ending but I'm not committing to anything, certainly nothing that involves danger on the high seas, especially in my current state -- halfway between messed up and oblivion."

"That's all for now. More tomorrow. I can't wait. You're going to think I've lost what's left of my mind."

"That's most encouraging. You certainly know how to instill confidence."

"Well, you're the only person who can make this happen and you're probably the only person who would even consider it."

"I have to turn in now before I come to my senses and catch the next flight home. Thanks for a wonderful dinner and bedtime story. If I'm gone in the morning, you'll know I've regretfully declined finding out any more about your so-called ending, which will probably end us both."

I patted Magic on the back as I slipped down through the hatch toward my assigned stateroom. I fell asleep in my clothes and slept through what was left of the night. My sleep was deep and hard and without nightmares. It had been a long time coming.

Chapter Seven

I awoke to the sound of a ship at sea, not tied up at the dock, but crashing through the ocean. I figured Magic had kidnapped me and was glad of it. The great rolling motion of the *Empress* encouraged me to lie back and snooze some more but I got up just to see where the hell Magic had taken me. One look through a porthole provided a sweeping view of the California coastline on the starboard side so I knew we were headed north. I pulled myself together and wandered topside.

As I came up through the hatch and spotted Magic at the helm, I was overcome by how invigorated I felt with the wind on my face. This morning it actually felt good to be alive, though I probably didn't look so hot after having slept in my clothes. I was unshaven, unshowered and a bit hung over, but my outlook was positively sunny.

"Am I being shanghaied?" I asked over the trawler's twin Cummins diesels.

"Not today. More planning is involved and you have to be a willing shanghai-ee. Right now, I can offer you a thermos of coffee before any further intrigue."

I gratefully accepted the hot coffee and did what I could as first mate though Magic was an accomplished captain. We didn't talk for a while. Silence had always come easy to us. We were comfortable with the quiet moments.

As Magic came about and headed the *Empress* home, it was clear he had more to say about what was on his mind. "About a year ago, right before I retired, I was back in Coronado when the duty officer knocked on my door and said there was a call from my daughter."

"Your what!"

"I know. All of SEAL Team One was giggling outside my door, which is as absurd an image as I can conjure. Anyway, I took the call, thinking it was a gag. The operator on the line sounded as if she were calling from the Moon, but it turns out she was in Thailand with a collect call for Admiral Black from his daughter.

"As you know, it's impossible to just call someone at Special Ops. All calls are secure and no names are given out, so I figured it had to be someone who knew me and didn't want to disclose her identity on a non-secure line. After accepting the call, I heard a young girl's voice, 'Dai uy, Bac Jim?'

"It was Gabe Freeman's daughter, Mai Lee, now all grown-up. He was in my SEAL team and he and I spent time with his Vietnamese family. She always called me Uncle or Bac Jim. She was just learning to talk when Gabe was killed in action. His best friend Trong, a Vietnamese SEAL in our team, and I tried to get his family out but failed. Trong wound up being captured and put in a re-education camp for 10 years, publicly disgraced, forced to do menial labor and finally let go. All I heard about Mai Lee was that she and her family were able to escape by boat to Thailand years later and wound up in a refugee camp there."

"I remember how hard you worked to find them before the Fall of Saigon in 1975, but everything was total chaos."

"Mai Lee had been trying to get hold of me for 14 months through the U.N., the Pentagon and God only knows what other government agency. Finally, using the deserted daughter ploy, she was able to get the number to the Amphib Base in Coronado. She knew me as a lieutenant but luckily someone realized that ranks change and put her through to me.

"Since I was retiring in less than 30 days, I took leave and hopped a series of MAC flights to find her. There are only four of them left: Mai Lee and her little brother Benny, who isn't so little now; his best friend Chien and Trong, Chien's father and Gabe's old teammate, who somehow found the three of them in the refugee camp. Mai Lee's mom and aunt died in the camp.

"Once I got there, I found out the whole miserable story. Mai Lee's family joined several other families and made their way to the coastal city of Vung Tau. There they procured a boat and sailed around the southern tip of Vietnam into the Gulf of Thailand where they were overtaken by Thai pirates, who killed all the males except for Benny and Chien, who were just kids. The SOBs only beat the kids unconscious. Benny's Vietnamese father was killed with the others and all the women were raped, including Mai Lee."

"Damn, Magic! I'm sorry."

"They would have probably all been killed had not an approaching British destroyer forced the pirates to flee. The remaining family members were taken to internment camps in Thailand."

"So what's going to happen to them now?'

"An excellent question, my friend. I sailed my beloved *Freedom* into a marina south of Bangkok and put Mai Lee and Benny onboard while I found a place for Trong and Chien nearby. It took some finagling with the Embassy and the Thai authorities but everything is copasetic for now until I can bring the kids to the States."

"Say no more. The teacup is yours, whatever it's worth. I think it's wonderful that you want to help this family. I've got enough money to live comfortably. You're the one who spent every waking hour finding out the teacup's true value. I would have never done all that work."

"That's a very wonderful offer, Beau, and I do appreciate your generosity, but I'm afraid I'm going to be asking for much more because I need much more. Priceless isn't what it used to be."

"So you didn't just fly me out here to have me sign away my rights to the teacup?" My mind was going to places I didn't want to visit but I couldn't control its mad mapping of places worlds away.

We had entered San Diego Harbor and were chugging our way toward the yacht club marina. The seagulls followed us, hoping that the trawler had brought home a bountiful catch but soon realized this was not the case. The harbor was busy with sail and motor boats, kayaks and rowing shells. Magic navigated through it all with ease.

The San Diego Harbor bore no resemblance to the low, wooded waters around my homeland. We entered from south to north with Point Loma's two lighthouses on the west. When I asked about the lighthouse redundancy, Magic said the one on top of the hill was built first but no one consulted the locals who knew that when the fog rolled in, the top of the hill was totally obscured, necessitating the addition of a beacon at sea level. Nothing beats local recon, I thought to myself.

Further up the channel, we passed the submarine base with its black humps protruding in the water, then the pens holding sea lions and dolphins used for mine detection and torpedo recovery – not my idea of job security. On the opposite side of the channel lay the North Island Naval Air Station with a runway that came right to the water's edge.

When Magic made the turn for the yacht harbor, I resumed my first-mate duties, putting out the fenders and getting the lines ready. As he maneuvered the *Empress* into her slip, I jumped to the dock and attached the spring line, then went back for the stern line and finally pulled up the bow. After the wash-down, we went below for scrambled eggs and more coffee.

"How about a jog around the island?" Magic asked as we cleared the table and cleaned up the galley. "Bet your butt hasn't been in gear in some time."

"You're just trying to wear me down until you can talk me into some hare-brained scheme. You know I hate jogging. How about loping? I can do loping."

As I changed clothes, I realized I still hadn't showered. No need now. I was just going to sweat some more. More deodorant – that was the ticket. I met Magic topside and we headed down the dock and out of the yacht club toward the harbor at Shelter Island. After a few Magic-led stretching exercises, we broke into a run, following the outside wall of the club until we reached Shelter Island Drive. This road ran down the isthmus and out onto the island, which fronted San Diego Bay with a welcoming park along the water's edge. In the distance, facing us head-on, was the aircraft carrier *USS Constellation*. No matter how many times I had seen America's might displayed in such massive splendor, I was always amazed by the sight, especially in international waters. Today, the armored flight deck was silent. What covered the space of 10 football fields was sparsely populated. Only a few planes and a couple of helos were visible. When underway at 20-plus knots (with tales of 30-plus sprints), 5000 souls and a full complement of fighter, attack and reconnaissance planes, she was a force to be reckoned with anywhere in the world.

I had stopped in my tracks for the past several minutes and was surprised that Magic wasn't giving me a hard time over my slacking.

But, no, he had pulled up too and was following my gaze.

"Sure was a kick in the pants, the life we led," Magic observed with a grin.

"We knew who we were, young and stupid, and we knew we had a mission and that there was someone to watch our backs."

"Thank God, we counted on each other, not the politicians, most of whom never saw a lick of action. What was that name we had for the rear echelon that outnumbered the front-line troops nine to one in Nam?"

"We gave them the respect they deserved – REMFs, Rear Echelon Mother Fuckers."

"It's a pity they never had the pleasure of our company."

We continued at a more leisurely pace. Loping seemed to have won the day, though my SEAL friend would never admit it. We paused again as we came upon the bronze monument to San Diego's tuna fishermen who had lost their lives at sea. The life-size, dark-patina statue depicted three fishermen, each with a cane pole, their lines tied to the same hook, which had been swallowed by a large tuna. When I first came to San Diego, tuna fishing was still done this way by the Italian- and Portuguese-descended fishermen. Men and poles were added for larger fish. A 400-pounder might need four guys with four poles. Once the chumming had put the fish in a feeding frenzy, the fishermen flipped a feathered, barb-less hook in the water with a man at one end jigging it.

When the big fish bit, all four men would lift it out of the water over their heads and a man on the other end would flip the tuna off the hook. Then back into the water for another fish. Much more efficient than the fishing Helen and I had accomplished on the *Blue Crab*. If we'd been living off our catch, we would have starved to death. It was good to be reminded of Helen by the good times and not just be haunted by the emptiness of days and the loneliness of nights.

We were now headed back, returning the same way we had come. As we neared the yacht club, Magic asked, "Beau, do you remember the jiggling jogger in Coronado?"

"Oh God, Magic!" I chortled. "That woman was going in all directions at once – a boomerang gone berserk." I hadn't thought about that in years. It also seemed as though I hadn't laughed in years.

Magic and I had returned from Vietnam and were jogging around the Coronado Amphib Base when approached by another jogger, this well-endowed young lady before the advent of sports bras. Just 10 yards ahead of us, she abruptly stopped her run to steady her breasts, to get them back in sync and regain her balance. She passed us a few seconds later as if nothing had happened. And thanks to our rigorous standards of military discipline, Magic and I maintained a straight face.

Our run done, we opted for showers at the club so we could take good, long ones and wound up at the bar for burgers and beer.

"Okay, I'm ready for anything," I confessed. "Tell me what's on your mind – why I'm here when I could be living my own perfectly miserable life in North Carolina."

"I'd like to make something right." There was a deep sigh and then he began again. "Mai Lee's family had neither money nor clout so they weren't included in the many Vietnamese allowed to immigrate to the U.S. after the war. And the fact that her father was a SEAL killed in action didn't seem to matter either. They were used up and left behind like obsolete machinery and they suffered terribly because of the help they provided the Americans."

"And the cup can't finance their resettlement needs now?"

"It's going to take more cups – for resettlement, legal costs, housing, schooling – a real shot at the American dream."

"So you want to go back to Vietnamese waters, try to find the original dive site, somehow uncover more treasure and do it all without getting caught."

"I have a plan," Magic interjected, a little too enthusiastically.

"I bet you do and it obviously includes me, which is frightening in itself. I've been out of the game for a long time."

"You still have all the necessary skills to make this thing happen. I can't do it without you. You're the best at what you do."

He was dead serious. His jaw was set and his somber eyes were fixed on a point beyond the horizon. I had seen this look before and had to admit it was still unnerving.

"Magic, I don't know what to say. Think about what you're proposing. I only found the one cup. The rest of the booty could be miles away from the original site, if I can find it. A dive operation, even if we looked like Vietnamese fishermen, which we don't, would attract the Vietnamese authorities and boat loads of pirates, and the operation could take forever. Hell, Mel Fisher, a professional treasure hunter with lots of help and sophisticated toys, found the Atocha in 1985 and the site is still being worked with much of the treasure as yet unfound. Surely there's a better way to help the Luongs.

"Beau, this is something I have to do and I have to do it now. There is no other way. I just want you to think about it."

I agreed to the thinking but not to the doing as we paid our tab, got up and headed back to the *Empress*.

Chapter Eight

The sun was setting as we stepped aboard the *Empress*. It was one of those spectacular displays of red, orange and purple swirls thanks to some cumulous clouds and hazy smog. We opted to sit topside for a while and watch the show, starting with coffee and moving right along to tequila.

As a child, I fantasized about sunken treasure -- gold doubloons, pieces of eight, precious jewels and silver chalices. These enchanting, shiny things didn't look so bright after centuries in the ocean. It took an expert to recognize the potential of rusted metal and jewels encrusted in coral. Gold and silver didn't rust and they could be vacuum-dredged without damage, but porcelain needed to be recovered by hand. It would be slow, painstaking work with no assurance of success. The only advantage to our treasure site was that the huge coral mound, where the original cup had been found, was a relatively small area to work if indeed it held more treasure.

Certifiable, incurable romantic that I was, I still thought Magic's idea was nuts. What kind of ship would we have to have to pull off this operation and yet not draw unwanted attention? Who would believe that two tall foreigners, one black and the other white, weren't worth at least a second look and possibly some enhanced questioning? Being a prisoner again in that part of the world gave me chills. All it would take to do us in would be a passing fisherman with a single-digit IQ.

As we sipped our second Patron, Magic turned his attention from the fading sunset to me and blessed my presence with his wise smile. He had that rare gift of making a person feel special, appreciated, worthy of his complete attention. Had he chosen to be a con artist or politician, he would have made millions. The only thing that could have stood in his way was his inability to suffer fools gladly or at all. But those he loved and respected were given all he had to give. He made his life's work to surprise people, to exceed expectations. Magic was only the second admiral in the Navy's history who achieved that rank as a SEAL. He led brilliantly and fearlessly, getting in and out of impossible situations with amazing skill, great success and few casualties – hence, the name Magic. Who was I to doubt his ability to pull off one more sleight of hand?

"All right, I'm in. I'm not sure why. Mostly, I think it's because I have to hear how you plan to pull this off and then I need to be there to make sure you get out alive."

Magic just smiled as if he had all the answers. Now that I was onboard, everything could move along as planned. I was more intrigued than reassured by Magic's sunny outlook. He appeared undeterred and started rolling out what he had obviously been researching for months.

"I knew you couldn't resist this one last bit of Magic. To begin with, finding the treasure is going to be easier than you think because the reef is the wreck."

"How could you possibly know that?"

"Reconnoiter, dear Watson. What we SEALs do best."

"What?"

"Six weeks ago, on my way to Thailand from Hong Kong, I sailed *Freedom* along the edge of Vietnamese territorial waters. I took a trusted friend with me, a Chinese history professor working for the Hong Kong Museum of History. Dr. Zhao, or Doc Wow as I call him, agreed to accompany me and to keep everything we discussed completely under wraps. He only asked that the museum be given a chance to buy one of the teacups should we find them, but I told him I couldn't promise anything and certainly didn't want to be hounded by Chinese authorities.

"Anyway, just as we neared Vietnamese jurisdiction, I took the precaution of radioing Hai Phong to alert authorities that *Freedom* had a bad water pump and that we needed to use the lee side of one of the outlying islands for cover while we fixed it.

"We were given permission for the repair, but we still got a visit from a patrol boat, which boarded and searched us. With our stated destination Bangkok and our promise to stay outside territorial waters, we allayed most of their suspicions. We also figured that a temperamental water pump would give us a running excuse for any other patrol boats that might spot us near the treasure site.

"We left the next day, continuing on course. We saw a few other patrol boats and planes but the surveillance waned. Once around the tip of Vietnam and into the Gulf of Thailand, we headed toward the treasure site you had shown me that one time. It's still just as remote as ever, just outside territorial waters. We arrived, as planned, at 2100 hours with no moon. The treasure site is a nice lee with a clear, safe approach. Zhao took the helm and I went diving with a metal detector which told me there's a lot of iron there – a ship's worth. I'd like to tell you that, in collecting chunks of corral, I came up with more cups, but that's not the case – just wood planking. The wreck is there, Beau.

"Anyway, after the dive, I checked out the nearby island in my black sneak-and-peek attire and found it deserted -- beautiful but uninhabited. And the next village is about 20 nautical miles south of the main island of Phu Quoc. It's all good."

"It's all good except for all the things you didn't mention," I pointed out, pouring myself another shot and hoping it would help anesthetize my rising misgivings. "You've been there but how do we get back, outfit a boat for the job that won't draw attention, blend in with the locals, get the treasure and get out in one piece?"

"I'm putting you in charge of boat operations and logistics. Get us there with the right vessel rigged to do the job – salvage gear, diving equipment, food, etc."

"The *Freedom* worked for reconnoiter but we need to get a boat out of Bangkok for re-outfitting, something that won't look out of place."

"Just what I was thinking," agreed Magic. "Did you ever read Ernest K. Gann's *Soldier of Fortune*? Great book -- Clark Gable starred in the movie."

"I do remember the story line. Gable signed on to help some woman find her husband who'd left Hong Kong to do a story on Communist China and was captured."

"Yeah, that's the one. Gable and the wife take a converted junk upriver to rescue him. Remember the junk?"

"No, not really."

"On the outside, the junk looked totally innocuous but the inside was all decked out with big engines and a Bofors cannon hidden in the bilges."

"So, Clark, you think we should convert a junk for this operation?" I asked sounding surprisingly reasonable as I felt myself succumbing to Magic's spell.

"Exactly. With your expertise with boats and God knows you've boarded enough vessels to be familiar with junks and all the contraband they can hide. You find us a seaworthy craft, fix it up for our purposes offshore and we're in business."

The challenge itself was intoxicating, made more so by the crema de cacti, the favored potion of outlaws and nectar of the gods, described so knowingly by author Tom Robbins. To re-design a vessel, enter foreign waters, operate undetected for a lengthy period of time and bring home treasure – now this was the stuff of last hurrahs.

We called it a night promising to get more of the details hammered out in the morning, knowing full well that anything planned tonight would be full of derring-do that would probably not end well.

As I drifted off, I was at the helm of a Chinese junk under a full set of lateen sails. Guiding me through the ocean were dolphins riding the bow.

Chapter Nine

By the time I'd awakened, there was coffee brewing and Magic had the main salon table covered with charts and catalogs.

As I sipped my first cup, I tried to see through the receding tequila haze and remember just what I'd promised Magic as he smiled at me across a sea of treasure-hunting paperwork.

"Don't worry, we're not in Vegas and you made no vows last night that can't be undone," Magic reassured me. "If you're all in, that's great. If you can just help me with the master plan, junk design, outfitting and operations, then that would be very much appreciated and I'll take it from there."

"You mean do all the work and let you have all the fun? No way, I'm just not sure I'm the asset you need for the cloak-and-dagger stuff."

"You've got a natural talent for covert operations. Why do you think the CIA made overtures to you right before you left the Navy? Those spooks recognized your gift to improvise, to think your way out of trouble on the fly. Perhaps, it's instinctive from your Southern upbringing, something from your seagulls-and-oysters knowledge bank."

"Aw shucks," I responded sarcastically, while secretly enjoying the bad pun. "You don't have to fill my head with images of James Bond. There's not enough tequila in Mexico to make me believe that crap. I'm no master spy but I can get you a boat ready and I can go diving for teacups with you. Just make damn sure we're not captured or killed – that's your job."

"If things get too hot, I'll back off and we'll head home," Magic promised.

"Deal," I agreed, knowing full well that circumstances often prevented such clear decision making -- that sometimes there was no safe way out.

"So we start with your going to Bangkok and buying the right junk. The *Freedom* is already there and Mai Lee and her brother Benny are keeping everything shipshape. Chien and Trong are nearby – good men you can trust. All of them are very able-bodied sailors and can help you find the best junk at the best price and then make sure you locate a very private cove to convert everything at sea. What do you need to go back with you and what should be shipped?"

"Hell, Magic, I don't know. I've never packed for a teacup rescue before. Suntan lotion, bug repellent, toothpaste, credit cards, cash, diving gear, copies of *Soldier of Fortune* and *Stranger in a Strange Land* -- pretty damn near everything, I guess. But before we get too far along here, I have to resolve not just how our boat will blend in with its surroundings, but how we'll actually pull off the diving without drawing attention."

For the next couple of days, Magic and I starting compiling a list of the gear, tools and supplies we'd need that weren't already onboard *Freedom*. In the evenings, we'd plot and scheme and try to think of everything that could go wrong, which was much too time-consuming for my taste. Worst-case scenarios always brought me back to the same question: What the hell was I thinking? Then again, what did I have to lose?

The best parts of our evenings were Magic's history lessons. He thought we should know all we could about Chinese junks and it wasn't long before we learned more than I ever wanted to know but still realized might come in handy in the re-design decisions.

By the second century AD, the Chinese were boldly taking their junks to sea and venturing throughout the Indian and Pacific Oceans. They even sailed as far as South Africa long before Vasco da Gama sailed his fleet from Lisbon around the Cape of Good Hope, discovering a southern route to India. As long as 400 feet, the treasure ships were only one of the many types of junks that were used to also transport troops, horses and supplies. They could be armed for fierce battles against pirates or other nations.

As Magic told his tales, I kept hoping we would fare better than many of the junk crews who were lost at sea. We would certainly have the willing, the able and a sense of shared purpose that was often missing on the ancient vessels. We'd also make good use of advancements in technology that could keep us safer. But I didn't discount the stories of how the earlier sailors put their faith in flying red flags for good luck to keep the dragon happy, the mythical dragon whose anger was manifested in typhoons. We would definitely be flying red flags.

With the lines of a stout dowager, the junk was amazingly efficient. She was the first vessel that could actually sail to windward. Some 15 percent of her sails were forward of the mast and all the sails operated like Venetian blinds made of bamboo-strip panels, battens, which were each attached to a line or sheet for trimming the sail. This meant that the sail could be trimmed differently at the top than at the bottom, increasing efficiency. The strong stern-mounted rudder, which took several men to steer, was put down the ship's center line through a watertight box bisecting the deck and hull. This meant the depth of the rudder could be changed depending on the depth of the water to maximize effectiveness and to minimize chances of running aground.

More importantly, from our perspective, junks possessed structure rigidity, making them extremely seaworthy. The junk was compartmentalized using waterproof bulkheads, both transversely and longitudinally, providing strength and protection from damage. For centuries, this combination of qualities made the Chinese junk the most seaworthy vessel in the world. It wasn't until the 1800s that Western naval design caught up.

With my head full of Chinese junk drawings and capabilities, I went searching for a shipwright to see if my latest idea for diving undetected might actually work. Since Magic had left for an appointment and turned his cell off and this job was too important to rely on the *Yellow Pages*, I thought it best to ask around the marinas. One name kept coming up as the go-to guy for building and repairing boats – Gustavo. I found Gustavo's shop on Harbor Island. When he came out to greet me, I was surprised by how young he was since many of his admirers had been old salts. Gustavo was in his mid-30s, clean-shaven with short, black curly hair. His shop was full of the tools of his trade and everything was shipshape. The smell of lumber, laminates and paints was accompanied by the sweetness of his cigar smoke.

"I heard you're the best shipwright around," I said as I shook his hand.

"Thank you. I come from a long line of shipbuilders who'd kick my ass if I ever did anything to sully the family name."

"That's good to know because I'm here for lessons and to do some prefab work. I'm afraid I don't have an actual vessel for you to work on. What I'm trying to do is see if what I have in mind can actually be done."

"I take that as a personal challenge," Gustavo replied excitedly.

We talked in broad terms about the project, settled on an hourly rate and got down to specifics about an at-sea ship conversion: proper tools, woodworking materials, new sealers and glues – it was a long list. This was the first of many sessions with Gustavo, who seemed to have an answer for everything, which was most comforting. More than one of my recent nightmares involved the junk taking on massive amounts of water and sinking. There was so much at stake and we would only have one shot at this.

To allay any fears of drug-running or human-trafficking, I fabricated a story about needing to do all this work in the process of shooting a film at a very remote location where I couldn't rely on local talent or material. Gustavo was quick to point out that he'd been a technical consultant on more than one production. I was in California after all.

Chapter Ten

With much to report to Magic about his suggestion of making a junk our base of operations, I suggested we have dinner at the Del. He was delighted with the idea. After all, the grand Hotel del Coronado had always been a favorite of ours and Helen's. I had taken her there on our first official date one arid Mediterranean-like summer evening when I already knew I was hopelessly smitten.

Driving over the Coronado Bay Bridge with its 90-degree bend and sweeping vistas of the sea and ships brought back more memories than I expected. Its 200-foot-high span, built to meet Navy specs for its huge ships, was still a rush. Once on Coronado Island, we headed down Orange Avenue straight for the Del, the elegant Victorian queen crowned by her glorious red roofs.

We found a quiet corner for dining in the Crown Room and ordered as though we were eating our last meal. Both of us knew we'd be roughing it for some time and, of course, there was the unspoken possibility we wouldn't be coming back. My appetite had returned with a vengeance and I ate everything but the centerpiece. Magic made a mighty effort at his steak but finally succumbed to defeat and vowed to take the remainder home for breakfast. We savored the moment as much as the food and relived some of the good times we'd had here in what seemed like a former lifetime.

After dinner, we meandered through the hotel grounds onto the beach for a walk. I figured I'd have to walk to L.A. to work off my dinner, but this was a start.

"I think I can make your junk idea work," I began. "The Vietnamese ply the shallow waters near the Mekong Delta to the edge of the 20-fathom mark. They use a combination of vessels from large sailing junks, which operate in pairs towing huge nets between them, to small sampans that run the narrow canals in the jungle. We should try to pass as a vessel from this eastern coast of Vietnam. Our junk has simply blown into the Gulf of Thailand to escape a nasty storm, which has caused a lot of damage. We had no choice but to anchor for repairs. The clannish locals will leave us alone and the authorities should not be immediately concerned with our presence."

"Damn, that would work! We're an incapacitated fishing junk. Of course, we're sailing in from Bangkok, Beau, so we're going to have to make a wide circle to look like we're coming in from the other direction. After we anchor near the treasure site, how do we pull off the diving?"

"The diving is a bigger challenge. It has to be done without anyone seeing a thing. Remember the Hughes Glomar Explorer, supposedly built for ocean mining, but used by the CIA to recover a sunken Soviet sub in 1974. The Glomar was able to pull the sub into its belly while Soviet ships encircled the vessel – so menacingly close and yet clueless. The belly was a moon pool, an internal underwater hangar with ocean access. That's what we need and a junk should be perfect for this with its compartmentalized structure. We prefab whatever we can, and when the time comes, cut a hole in the bottom of the junk for our dives. This moon pool can also serve as a hiding place for the two of us should we be boarded. Our Vietnamese crew will know what to say while we're sitting in one of the watertight storage vaults built into the pool. The diving equipment and any found treasure must be stowed there as well. We'll have what we need to survive in our hideaway, though we may miss happy hour. From above and below, the moon pool will just look like a ship taking on water from a gash in the hull. We'll work out signals so we'll know if anything is wrong when we're coming up from a dive, though I think we'll be able to spot intruders from below."

"Genius, sheer genius!" trumpeted Magic, "I knew you could pull this off."

"It's going to be tricky. I'll try not to sink us. I'd like to do all the construction work in one fell swoop, but I think it's wise to wait to cut out the moon pool until we anchor, since our junk may no longer be very seaworthy once the hull is breached."

"So we need back-up troop and treasure transport," Magic chimed in – always a step ahead. Grasping how complicated everything is becoming, he chooses himself a comfortable-looking sand dune and takes a seat. I join him on a matching perch.

"I think we can buy enough time to find the treasure without sinking, if the weather holds, but I'd recommend that we abandon and scuttle her and rely on inflatables to get us back to wherever you position *Freedom* in international waters. A 16-foot Zodiac with a 50-hp outboard could carry six people plus several hundred pounds of treasure at 25-plus knots for more than 100 miles. We leave fast, under the radar and without a trace of our skullduggery."

"That's the way I want this thing to end for all our sakes."

"And don't forget we'll have more teacups than the Queen of England," I added holding up my right hand with a pretend cup of tea, realizing too late that my abbreviated pinky finger wasn't very well suited for snooty posturing.

"Wish I had gotten there a little sooner," lamented Magic. "You would probably be invited to more teas."

"Yea, the tea thing is a real shame. What's important is that you got there and I still have the rest of me, including my trigger finger, which may be of much greater importance in our upcoming enterprise. You do have some source for weapons?"

"They're already onboard *Freedom*. I took a couple with me and Trong procured a few more. He's a good man. I've been on ops with him and he's very resourceful and rock-steady under fire."

“So we have a crew of six we can count on – four for the junk and two to sail *Freedom*. We’re stretched thin but we have all the skills we need: native speakers, sailors, divers and trained survivors. I just hope they’re good cooks.”

“And you’re going to have to be a supreme negotiator for the junk because you’ll probably be dealing with a pirate kingpin.”

“Have you already sold the first cup to bankroll this operation ‘cause it’s not going to be cheap?”

“No worries, mate, I have it all covered.”

“You’re holding on to the teacup, aren’t you? Just in case that’s all you have to give Mai Lee and Benny.”

“I don’t want to touch that yet. I have plenty of my own money -- more than enough to last me.” Magic stood up, brushed the sand off his trousers and waited for me to join him.

This was an odd statement I thought, one I’d never been able to make. We walked back toward the lights of the Del, both deep in our own thoughts.

Chapter Eleven

The next morning, Magic and I visited Gustavo to see how he was coming on the prefab work. The two of them already knew each other from repairs done on *Empress*. We collected all the supplies and parts that were ready and Magic arranged with Gustavo to follow-up on any odds and ends that might be needed over the coming weeks. I had briefed Magic on the movie-making cover story and he continued the subterfuge – just another day in the life of a special ops guy.

We were calling the prep work a wrap, since we had checked off most of our long list. It was time to actually put our plan in motion. A day of phone calls and faxes took care of all my personal needs prior to departing. My North Carolina friends and neighbors sounded relieved and happy for me to be taking a long trip with a friend. My island home was in good hands and was most likely receiving better care now than I had provided since Helen's death. My lawyer-friend already had my power of attorney and was happy to overnight my passport. No visa was required for Thailand for up to 30 days and there was a 10-day extension available if needed. Overstaying our welcome would probably mean we were in jail, visa or no visa.

Magic organized the flights and had his "daughter" begin the search for a junk in Bangkok. I shopped for all the last-minute things I kept adding to the list as some kind of subliminal stalling technique.

Magic and I continued our workouts, but he seemed less driven about fitness and more focused on the job ahead. We were both having second thoughts – what I called the looking before the leaping, which was always the point of no return. As always, Magic was more worried about putting his team at risk than his own personal safety.

It had been decided early on that I would leave first, meet Mai Lee and inspect the junks she believed to have potential. Magic would follow in a few days, finishing up his own checklist and forwarding extra parts, equipment or any other damn thing we'd forgotten.

Before I headed for the airport, Magic and I hit the bar at the yacht club one last time. As in Nam, I was the one shipping out first and Magic hosted the sendoff – this time with martinis. As the first of several arrived, Magic lapsed into his Ogden Nash:

"There's something about a Martini,
A tingle remarkably pleasant;
A yellow, a mellow Martini;
I wish that I had one at present.
There is something about a Martini,
Ere the dining and dancing begin,
And to tell you the truth –
It is not the vermouth –
I think that perhaps it's the gin."

Raising his glass to meet mine, Magic pronounced, “One’s too many and three’s not enough. Here’s to going boldly forth, my friend. ”

“And returning to tell the tale,” I added.

The martinis flowed and were accompanied by some yummy munchies. Finally, the taxi arrived and I poured myself into it. I was off to Bangkok via Los Angeles on the red-eye.

I made my connection in L.A. and sat back in my first-class seat, which though comfortable for now, would become old after 17 hours. I wasn’t sure whether I was excited about this highly improbable treasure hunt or just relieved not to be back on my island, where everything reminded me of Helen. It was good to be of use to someone, even if it was a slightly mad ex-SEAL with his one last Hail Mary mission. When the seat next to me remained empty, allowing me to stretch out my long frame, I took it as an auspicious omen.

Chapter Twelve

I didn't so much sleep as pass out on my flight into Bangkok. It wasn't just the martinis; it was emotional and physical exhaustion. Magic and I had been going non-stop since my arrival, trying to get our head around an irrational idea, convincing ourselves it could be done and then pulling all the pieces together.

The smell of fresh coffee and sunlight though the windows awakened me. I felt surprisingly good for sleeping on an airplane. I had lost a day, I remembered, but then I'd lost a lot of days over the past year. With coffee, I opted for a Thai breakfast, including vegetables, rice and hot chilies. Though I'd never been to Thailand before, I'd heard that the chilies were introduced by the Portuguese traders returning from South America in the 1500s and that these chilies had given Thai food its distinctive spiciness ever since. I was game.

On our approach into Bangkok's Don Mueang International Airport, I could see the ribbon of the Chao Phraya River running through the sprawling city below. The massive high rises jutted out from the river basin and the tallest among them, the Baiyoke Tower II, stood prouder than the rest with its 85 stories. However, they didn't compare in grandeur to the Buddhist temple spires standing guard over the city, and Wat Arun, the Temple of Dawn, appeared to be the mightiest defender of them all. In shorthand Thai, Bangkok was Krug Thep, meaning city of angels, so I took this as another good sign. We were going to need all the angels we could get.

On my first trip to Southeast Asia, I had been introduced to the sweltering tropics by a rush of superheated air the moment the plane opened its doors. Not today; not in Bangkok. I was welcomed by air-conditioning, given a polite once-over by Customs and Immigration and introduced to Don Mueang, one of the world's oldest and busiest international airports, now spread out before me in a throbbing scene of organized chaos. It was jarring to all my senses and overwhelming to my inner resolve that there was a really good reason for me to be here in the first place. Acclimating to all the sights, sounds and smells would come, I knew, but I was unprepared for all the memories of Southeast Asia that came rushing toward me like the airport crowds.

I tried to remember what Magic had told me. His comforting words came back to me, "Go to ground transport and Mai Lee will meet you there. She has all your arrival info and a rough description. It will be easier if she finds you, since you'll probably stand out, even with all the Western males coming in for the red-light district promises. Try not to look like some pree-vert. Mai Lee will be calling you Bac Beau. She'll come in the old Rover and then you'll have the ride of your life to the yacht club."

As I pushed my loaded luggage cart toward the exit, I heard my first "Bac Beau" and turned to meet Mai Lee. She was an exquisite woman-child with a white orchid in her long, black hair. She extended her hand, took mine, checked out its four-and-a-half digits and kissed my wrist before giving me a big hug. Only about five feet, she seemed taller because of her erect, regal bearing. With her golden eyes, she held my gaze as if sizing me up against the Magic lore. I asked her not to believe everything Magic had told her and she smiled. It was in the warmth of that smile that all my misgivings evaporated.

Chapter Thirteen

The woman in the tan suit had been following the Amerasian girl every chance she could over the past few weeks. While not an actual field agent, the Suit had gone through extensive training at "The Farm." Her primary job with the CIA in Bangkok was to stay on top of political, economic and cultural affairs, mainly through her skills as an interpreter. It was a posting she was born to pursue. Her Latino father had named her Isabella and taught her Spanish, but her Thai mother had insisted that she be raised in a traditional Thai household with its requisite language, culture and customs. Her childhood in America had given her the freedom to enjoy both backgrounds and become her own person.

Isabella's father had been a Marine captain attached to the American Embassy in Bangkok when he met her mother, an English teacher who worked part-time as an embassy staff tutor. From this union, Isabella inherited her exotic good looks – raven hair, olive complexion and dark almond eyes.

Professionally, her fluency in four languages and her degree in Asian studies would have made her a highly sought-after recruit in the public or private sector, but she chose the CIA. Her travels with the agency had taken her throughout Southeast Asia and landed her presently in Bangkok. Much of the population throughout the region was Tai: the Siamese, or

Thai, as well as the Shan in Northwest Burma (now Myanmar), the Lao in Laos and Northern Thailand, the Yunnan Tai in northern Vietnam and the Lü in Yunnan and Burma. Thai was spoken by all and much of what Isabella had learned in talking to her sources concerned the drug trade.

Drug production was controlled by war lords on the Burma-China border. The hill tribesmen growers could be found in the Shan States of Burma, Laos and Thailand. Khun Sa, the "Opium King," and other war lords, many of Chinese origin, controlled the harvests, transport and distribution. By paying off civilian and military officials, Thai mafia groups received protection for their drug shipments passing through the country to international markets. Bangkok served as a hub for much of this trade.

The drug trade was not a primary focus of the CIA except when drug money funded terrorist activities around the world. Certainly, illegal drugs had nothing to do with Isabella's assignment, but she had taken it upon herself to try to uncover the north-south drug routes. What the CIA was much more interested in was China's growing influence in the area. The Chinese were the second largest ethnic group in the country and were an integral part of Thai life, particularly in Bangkok. Isabella's Thai and Chinese language skills had helped her secure her current posting but she felt she could do so much more than act as an interpreter. She wanted to be seen as a skilled analyst and get herself promoted to field work by uncovering the major players in the drug trade.

During her four years in Thailand, Isabella had gathered information that pointed her to a Bangkok businessman named Wu in Bangkok. He ran restaurants, brothels and water and land taxis, as well as a small domestic cargo airline. All were legal, profitable and explained his frequent trips throughout the country and abroad. Isabella was most interested in his fleet of old fishing junks that she thought were perfect for smuggling drugs. Smuggling was a way of life in Southeast Asia. Everything from guns to sewing machines could be contraband. Many of the old fishing junks had once been pirate ships, engaged in chasing down and robbing refugees like the Vietnamese escaping after the war. Isabella had read accounts of these Thai pirates commandeering junks and sampans, beating the men, raping the women, killing everyone, including children. These boat people just disappeared along with all their worldly possessions.

Perhaps, it was these stories that made Isabella take notice of the young Amerasian woman who visited Li Wu's deteriorating junk fleet. While eating her lunch at a restaurant upriver as cover for watching Wu's junk business, Isabella had seen this woman come and go several times. It was the only thing of interest Isabella had come across in her patchy surveillance activities and so she followed her back to the Ocean Marina

Yacht Club near Pattaya Beach – over an hour's drive south of Bangkok.

Pattaya, once a small fishing village on the Gulf of Thailand, had reinvented itself into an upscale beach resort after the first American servicemen had ventured there on R&R from Vietnam. Now it was home to many Thai-Chinese, retirees from Europe escaping the high cost of living in their homelands and poor service workers from the Northeast.

Isabella followed her person-of-interest from the club parking lot into the huge marina where she watched her until she boarded a beautiful, U.S.-flagged yacht named *Freedom*.

Even an inexperienced spy knew where to gather information, so Isabella quickly turned her attention to finding the yacht club bar. After traversing the fountain-filled, high-domed gorgeous hotel lobby, she found the Harbour Lounge with it sweeping ocean views and took a seat at the grand circular mahogany bar. She was immediately welcomed by the Australian bartender Liam, who was more than happy to have such a lovely distraction to his uneventful day. Isabella asked Liam enough about his background to show much more interest than she actually had in the man. When she mentioned *Freedom*, Liam was not surprised.

"It's the envy of every sailor in the club," Liam said while placing some munchies in front of her. "Of course, most wouldn't want to do all the sanding and varnishing it takes to keep her up the way they do."

"I'd really like to meet the owner to see if I can arrange a charter," Isabella lied.

"I met him once when he first pulled in but I think he's back in the States. I remember he liked martinis. Big black American guy named Magic. Sorry, I can't arrange a meeting. Perhaps, one of the other skippers can help you. What did you have in mind – sailing, diving?"

"I guess I was just mesmerized by the thought of a sail on that yacht but I know there are others. I have to be getting back into the city but I'll be back," she winked.

Liam knew exactly what Isabella meant about being mesmerized. It took him several moments to regain himself and get back to work.

While driving back to Bangkok, Isabella thought she had made some progress in connecting Wu to his visitor from the yacht club but she had no idea what it all meant. Why would a woman with access to *Freedom* have any interest in an ugly, smelly and possibly unseaworthy junk? She reasoned that spare-time sleuthing was better than none at all. How would she ever become a real field operative if she was stuck behind a desk? She vowed to find out more about whatever was going on. This would require splitting her surveillance and not being made. She figured she could pull that off. How difficult could it be?

Within a week, she had somehow managed to be in the right place at the right time and had tracked her mysterious young woman from Wu's establishment to Don Mueang International where she picked up an arriving passenger, whom Isabella photographed and would later try to identify from immigration records.

Chapter Fourteen

Out of the airport and into Bangkok with Mai Lee at the wheel was a lot like out of the frying pan and into the fire. The traffic did not so much flow as convulse in pitching spasms and stomach-churning zigzags accompanied by continuous horn-blowing. There were minibuses, water and land taxis of every description and infamous tuk-tuks, the open-air rickshaw affairs used to separate the tourists from their money and introduce them firsthand to the choking pollution of the city. We had the Rover's windows down and sunroof open, and somewhere amid the petrol smells, I detected whiffs of turmeric, coriander and curry. There were restaurants and flower vendors everywhere and lots of open-air markets, even floating ones along the many brownish khlongs or canals crisscrossing the city. Through the roof, I could see sky circled by tall buildings on every side and stretches of the Skytrain.

"Forgive me, Bac Beau, you are getting the 25-cent tour as opposed to the nickel tour."

I laughed at her American expression. "I just appreciate your picking me up. I probably wouldn't have lasted too much longer in the throngs back there and I wouldn't want to be driving now. My survival training never prepared me for all this."

"I think someone was following me when I left the junk docks and I'm doing everything I can to give them the slip."

"Well, in that case, carry on," I chirped as we narrowly missed another truck and came face-to-face with an elephant in the middle of the street. Mai Lee zoomed around the unflappable beast and we took several more quick turns before she seemed content to start heading toward our destination, though she checked the rearview constantly.

"Bac Jim told me you'd provide a unique introduction to Bangkok. He seems to think you drive like this all the time."

"If you don't believe all his stories about me, I'll do the same for you."

"Deal," I agreed, trying hard to take in everything I was seeing – all the people, the colors, the modern city and the ancient temples.

"Benny and I were sorry to hear about your wife. Bac Jim loved Helen very much and talked about her. We know how talented she was."

"How's that?"

"One of her paintings hangs in the salon of *Freedom*. Her work is beautiful. I love all the colors and the peace she brings through her art."

"Thank you, Mai Lee. Helen would be touched by your praise."

The passing scene was turning more rural and fields were green indicating some welcome early rains. The mostly flat landscape was checker-boarded by cultivated pineapple and cassava fields with a few rice paddies sustained by intricate, interlacing irrigation systems. Small businesses and some humble homes planted themselves among the farms. It was warm and humid but a slight ocean breeze made for a good introduction to my new surroundings. We had left Highway 7 and were heading south on Sukumvit Road where palm trees greeted us from all directions. We would follow this road all the way into the marina.

Mai Lee asked about how Magic was doing and when he was coming. She then settled into her tour-guide mode telling me how Central Thailand was considered the rice bowl of Asia and had literally fed the economic development of the country since the 13th century.

"Do you miss Vietnam?" I asked.

"I do. It will always be my home but there's so much sadness in my memories. I'm trying to start over with Bac Jim's help. I want to go to college and be a doctor. Benny hopes to become an engineer. Perhaps, in America. Our English is good, yes?"

"Your English is better than most native speakers."

Mai Lee was pleased with this compliment. "What do I need to do to sound like you?"

"We'll work on your Southern drawl, if you like, but it's optional in most states."

"I like the idea of options."

"You're so young you should have a whole world of options to be anyone, do anything, go anywhere. That's what Bac Jim is trying to make happen."

"And now we begin," Mai Lee declared as she entered the Ocean Marina Yacht Club at Jomtien Beach south of Pattaya.

A full 24 hours after leaving San Diego, I arrived in another marina halfway around the world filled with an impressive array of vessels flying flags from at least a dozen different countries. Beyond the boats stretched the beckoning iridescent green-blue Gulf of Thailand. I tried to take it all in -- where I was, what I planned to do and how the hell I had come to this point in my life. Strangely, it seemed as if everything was exactly as it was meant to be.

After unloading the car and stowing the gear, I settled into life aboard *Freedom*. She was a beauty of a boat, lovingly cared for with the exacting attention to detail that only comes from truly dedicated sailors. Designed for the long sea voyage by Kauffman & Ladd, the Skye 51 was comfortable, functional and elegant – all at the same time. She was ketch-rigged with a fiberglass hull and teak deck. The 65-foot mainmast flew Old Glory and the Thai flag.

As I took the tour, I realized that *Freedom* was the embodiment of wabi-sabi, the revered Japanese tenet which espoused that certain objects had a spiritual hold on us through our acceptance that nothing lasts, nothing is finished and nothing is perfect. Within the concept of wabi-sabi, an individual finds some serenity in the realization of a fleeting connection, a longing not fulfilled but acknowledged and appreciated. This powerful, ephemeral attachment to a thing of beauty made this weary traveler feel right at home on *Freedom*. I was thankful for the momentary sense of peace that came from being cradled lovingly on life's sea rather than floundering in an ugly world. It was the same inner tranquility that filled my melancholy soul when I gazed at Helen's work.

Helen's painting hung in a place of honor in the salon. It was a scene captured on our island. I remembered watching Helen work her magic one stroke after another, layering colors, softening edges, brightening sunlight on the water. On this day, she had taken her easel outside and was moving like a dancer transferring paints from her palette to the canvas. She was always dressed in the same bright colors she lavished on her paintings and she put all her passion for life in each piece and this always came through. It was comforting to know she was onboard.

At Mai Lee's suggestion, I used the club's pool to work out the kinks from the flight. Afterward, we went to the bar for drinks and miang kham, a tasty assortment of ginger, coconut and dried shrimp served with a syrup sauce. Then we tried the oysters made unforgettable by the famous sri racha pepper sauce. Thai sauces ranged from hot to nuclear and went down best with chilled Singha beer. I remembered how Helen always said, "presentation is everything" as I studied and then ate the beautifully carved fruits and vegetables that seemed to adorn every dish.

I was enjoying my second beer when Mai Lee's younger brother showed up. He had just returned from a dive with two of his friends on one of the many wrecks in Pattaya waters. This day he'd spent time exploring the HTMS Khram, a Thai navy vessel just 15 meters below the surface. Introductions were made and diving stories swapped. Benny explained how there had once been incredible offshore reefs but they had been destroyed by dynamite fishing. He found the wrecks fascinating because of the stories they could tell. This was as close as we came to talking about why we were all here.

Binh Luong, Benny to everyone, was a good-looking young man with an easy smile in contrast to his somewhat more regal, reserved sister. Any questions I might have had about the two of them as crew were completely dispelled. I found myself falling easily into the role of Bac Beau, already feeling very protective of these two.

We headed back to *Freedom* where we could talk in private and put together a plan for the days ahead. We had a lot to do.

Mai Lee and Benny told me what they'd done to prepare *Freedom* for the mission and wanted to know their next assignments. They said that Chien and Trong were nearby and could be ready to move on a moment's notice. Mai Lee was so much the grown-up while Benny was still a kid, a good kid, but still a kid. He was also a hard worker and a quick learner according to Magic.

We decided to take a day for me to recover from my flight and to pull together what was already onboard *Freedom* with what I'd brought or ordered and to figure out what equipment and supplies we still needed. The following day, Mai Lee and I would go junk shopping.

Once we chose our vessel, Mai Lee and Benny thought we should immediately sail it to some remote islands in Southern Thailand just off that narrow strip of the country bordering Malaysia. We could work on the junk there and sail across the Gulf of Thailand straight for the treasure site from that point. It was reassuring to know that Mai Lee and Benny had already thought this through. They pulled out the map and showed me their proposed charted course. It was a great idea. Once we set sail for the site, it would look as if we were headed back to the fishing grounds where we should have originated before we were blown off course.

An at-sea rendezvous with *Freedom* to transfer people, equipment and gear could be tricky at night. A moonless sky, a little sea mist and well-coded and very sparse communications would be essential to having both vessels just disappear for a while. At no point was there to be any sign when *Freedom* was planning to depart. The slip was reserved for the next couple of months with notice that she'd be in and out.

My initial inspection of *Freedom's* assets led me to believe she had the necessary communications (Icom 700 single-sideband/ham radio and VHF-FM radio, Sony portable shortwave radio and Iridium satellite phone) and was generally well-equipped with most of the conversion tools we'd need and the essential dive gear. Her dive compressor was smaller than I liked, a 3.5CFM Bauer, but with a couple of large storage bottles and a storage tank, we'd be fine for hookah diving. Transferring the compressor, spare parts and dive gear was going to be difficult work. Of course, moving heavy equipment around boats, especially sailboats, was always a nightmare. Not only were we going to have to hide or disguise the compressor, we needed to supply it with clean outside air. I couldn't figure all this out until we actually had a junk and saw how it was laid out. Somehow it had to look like a fishing vessel, a distressed one at that, while functioning as a dive boat and a treasure-recovery unit. My mind was racing but my body was flagging and there came a point when I couldn't complete a sentence. Mai Lee and Benny sent me off to bed and I crashed, sleeping fitfully, dreaming of Trojan Horses.

Chapter Fifteen

Bordering the Chao Phraya River, the original Port of Bangkok and its newer, deep-water cousin and now Bangkok's major port, the Port of Laem Chabang, were cities unto themselves, alive with the modern wonder of massive cranes, huge container and cruise ships and miles of warehouses populated with thousands of dock workers, saffron-robed monks and street vendors.

Mai Lee and I made our way through the truckers, past the noisy markets and headed to the oldest section on the seediest side of the Bangkok Docks (Klong Toey). When I first got a feel for our destination, I was upset that Magic and I had sent Mai Lee into this place alone but quickly realized she was the best person for the job. I half expected an Asian Marlon Brando to come shuffling around the corner. This was a mob-movie setting waiting to be filmed -- just the kind of dark, dilapidated warren of buildings where people and contraband disappeared without a trace. The junks lined the docks, all in varying stages of decay. They looked and smelled like the ones I'd boarded and searched along the coast of Vietnam. Some were old enough to actually be the same junks. It was a far cry from the yacht club.

Our meeting was with a Chinese businessman/criminal named Wu, whose very name made Mai Lee cringe. She believed him to be more than capable of the same kind of larceny, rape and murder that had destroyed her family. In her dark musings about Wu, she had her own thoughts about the history of these junks -- that one of them could have been the pirate ship that boarded her family's boat and changed their lives forever.

Wu was expecting us. He was everything I had anticipated, almost a caricature of the Oriental villain of old Saturday matinees – a cross between Sydney Greenstreet in *The Maltese Falcon* and an evil Charlie Chan. Long black hair, swirled over a balding head, crowned a face of intense, watchful eyes and fat jowls highlighted by two gold teeth. As he smoked his cigarette in an ivory holder, he sized me up and tried to make some sense of what I wanted with a fishing junk. Rising to his feet with an unexpected easy grace considering his ample body, Wu adjusted his rumpled white suit and shook my hand with a strong, firm grip -- never taking his eyes off mine. This was a predator searching for vulnerabilities in his prey. It would not be pleasant to be at this man's mercy.

With a sharp command, Wu summoned his men, seemingly from nowhere, to point us in the right direction while he walked alongside us only to the end of the dock.

"Let me know if you find boat you like," he said as he stood by the gangway, close enough to see our discomfort with the smell of rotten fish and general filth, but far enough away not to have to experience it himself.

We looked at the two junks Mai Lee had chosen earlier. They swayed haphazardly in the middle of their orphaned kin, junks that had plied waters along the South Malay Peninsula and the eastern shores of Vietnam's Ca Mau Peninsula.

One junk was actually built out of teak but the other was so grimy I couldn't identify the wood. I checked the planking and frames with a penknife, looking for rot. The teak vessel seemed the better of the two. She was approximately 75-feet long with classic lateen sails in need of repair. She had a hand windless for cranking the wood anchor, which was weighted with rocks as the Chinese had done for 2000 years. The flukes were carved out of wood tied to a rock with a hole drilled in it to sink the anchor. The cargo hold was large and covered with fish scales and a foot of bilge water. I asked that the bilges be pumped dry. One of Wu's men returned quickly with a portable pump, something we would definitely have onboard. The bilge was no more attractive dry and smelled worse, but the garboard strake planks felt good. Since these planks intersected with the keel, they were a good indication of loose or weak keel bolts -- at least that was my hope. Under all the years of neglect, it appeared the junk had been well-built with good woods. It was outfitted with an old Gardner engine, which sounded like it could do the job once the crew got it started.

Finally, Mai Lee and I had seen enough. She was quick to point out details I missed and together we thought we'd given the junk a good once-over, sufficient enough to make an offer.

"How much?" I asked Wu as we rejoined him on the dock.

"What you want smelly junk for?"

"It's for a small movie, more a documentary than a feature, at least for now."

"400,000 baht," he replied flatly.

"I'm not talking Hollywood big-time studio here," I countered. "And I was thinking dollars."

"Dollars would be better. Then $10,000 would be good deal."

"Guess we should keep looking for one less smelly and less costly. Thanks for your time." I took Mai Lee's arm and turned to walk.

"How 'bout with new engine?" Wu offered.

"Let's see."

We followed Wu to a shed behind his office where he had another Gardner, still in the crate and covered in cosmoline. When the engine was uncrated, I pulled down the pressure release and used a large spanner to turn the fly wheel, which spun easily and smoothly. This old engine was actually brand new and was worth the price of the junk.

"OK, deal, $10,000 cash with this engine in place, ownership paperwork and harbor clearance all arranged and ready to go upon final payment. I have $3,000 to put down as a deposit."

"Deal," agreed Wu, thinking that he should have squeezed me for more, something he always fretted about, no matter how favorable the terms.

We shook hands and talked about the next meeting when the deal would be completed and the junk would set sail.

Chapter Sixteen

From the restaurant, Isabella watched Mai Lee and the tall man, whom she had identified as Beaufort MacEvoy, an American, talking with Wu. What were they doing? After a tour of those rancid junks, they were making some kind of deal and exchanging money. She grabbed her bag and pulled out a camera with telephoto lens. Sure enough, she was clearly witnessing some kind of payoff in U.S. currency. This could be big, she thought, before realizing how obvious her surveillance had become. She then turned her camera to other boats along the river and clicked away, but it was too late. Her waiter had noticed her from her earliest visits to his restaurant. Isabella's beauty and style of dress had made an impression on him. She was not his usual customer and she wasn't there for the food, barely touching her numerous meals. Sitting at the same table, she always seemed a little too interested in the least picturesque of the old docks. Today, she was more obvious than usual, and when she started taking pictures of Wu's business dealings, the waiter knew he had a valuable piece of information.

Betting that what he had just witnessed would be worth much more than he'd earn on this slow day at the restaurant, the waiter feigned illness and left. He immediately bicycled across the river and through several back streets to arrive at Wu's shipyard from a direction that could not be observed from the restaurant. Knowing he would never get an audience with Wu, he approached his driver. If his information was of no value, he didn't want to risk the wrath of Wu, which was known to rain down bodies along a wide swath of Bangkok.

The driver was menacing enough, frightening the waiter to pour out his observations like a long-overdue confession. The waiter was then moved up the chain of command and wound up in Wu's office with a young, muscular man with a shaved head, who took charge. Telling his story once again, the waiter was becoming more alarmed by the moment. He wondered if they were looking for holes in his narrative, so they could put holes in him. The bald man nodded to the driver, who left quickly, and then turned his attention back to the waiter, who wished fervently that he were back at the restaurant minding his own business. When the bald man was certain that the waiter thought he was about to die, he pulled 1,000 baht from his thick money clip and handed the bills to the waiter, promising him more should he see anything else of interest.

Wu's driver had immediately checked with locals who hung out around the restaurant and found more than one who remembered the woman, her car and its American Embassy plates. They were rewarded generously for their powers of observation. Within an hour, Wu had a description, a place of employment and a growing concern. Two Americans interested in Wu's business in one day were two too many. He assigned one of his best men to tail this woman and started making inquiries about his junk buyer. Were these two working together? His gut told him no because he thought the buyer was up to something himself, something that would not survive State Department scrutiny.

Chapter Seventeen

One of the most important things I learned in combat was that, when things were going too well, something was about to go wrong. I had a terrible sense that I was going to have to learn this lesson again. In Thailand for only a few days, I could report to Magic that we had a junk, a thoroughly briefed crew, the necessary equipment and the makings of a very workable plan for getting out to sea, disappearing, converting the junk and heading for treasure.

As I went over last-minute details with Magic, he sensed this nervousness.

“Beau, go talk to Trong. On more than one OP, he *listened* me into a good decision.”

In the seniority structure of the military, many a young officer was guided out of the quagmire of a new command by an experienced enlisted man who could give advice while appearing to simply listen.

Benny and I took the Zodiac up the coast to pick up Trong, who was staying with his son Chien, Benny’s best friend, until we were ready to sail. I dropped off Benny to visit with Chien while Trong and I just put-putted around for a while. I talked. He listened. It’s amazing how much faster things come together when they’re said out loud.

Trong was surprisingly tall for a Vietnamese. He was fit and carried himself well, revealing his military background. His handsome chiseled face was framed by his high cheekbones and lit up by his bright, aware eyes. He was indeed a good sounding board and he added options and presented solutions. I quickly realized that Trong would be indispensable to our mission.

Addressing my concerns, we devised a plan for our departure. There was no way we could change or disguise my appearance, so we decided to use it. I would be very visible aboard the junk as we motored downriver from Bangkok to the Gulf of Thailand. Trong would act as first mate and film cameraman to keep our cover story afloat. Our plan was to lose ourselves in the dark among the squid fishing fleet that sailed with the evening tide, relying on their spotlights and any fish-finders they might have.

Meanwhile Mai Lee, Benny and Chien would prepare *Freedom* to get underway for a cruise of the islands, retaining the slip at the yacht club for the ship's return – everything done with as little fanfare as possible. *Freedom* would leave a few days after the junk's departure, just in case anyone was starting to put things together.

We would rendezvous on the west side of Koh Phangan and continue to the small islands around Koh Phaluai, the largest of the 42 islands within Mu Ko Ang Thong National Marine Park, 250 square kilometers of which only about 20% was land. Once we found the most secluded island imaginable, we'd transfer equipment to the junk under the cover of darkness.

For communications, we'd carry VHF-FM radios. Trong and Mai Lee would communicate only in Vietnamese, and as an added precaution, had devised a code for critical information like rendezvous points. We also established seemingly random check-in times each day. The only problem with our communications would be *Freedom's* speed. She'd have to hold back and not outdistance the junk by too much, since our radios operated on line-of-sight. Under optimal conditions, signals might reach 100 nautical miles but were dependable only at a range of 10 to 15 miles.

It all sounded good, at least to Trong and me on that warm, sunny day skipping along the water just off the coast of the seemingly carefree resort town of Pattaya.

Chapter Eighteen

Arranging to meet Wu around noon, Trong and I hitched a ride in the Rover with Mai Lee. We had the gear we'd need to get the junk's motor and sails operational and to handle whatever emergency we thought we might encounter, including a Zodiac, if everything went wrong. The most conspicuous piece was probably the most useless except for maintaining our cover story -- the 16-mm Arriflex ST that I'd experimented with in making short videos back home. After using the filming cover story in San Diego, I thought it might come in handy here so I had a friend ship me the camera, which Trong would carry onboard in full view.

No one said much on the way. We were going to finalize a deal with the devil and we all knew it could go sideways in a hurry. I had opted to arm myself and stuck a .38-caliber pistol against the small of my back inside my jeans covered by a loose shirt. It wasn't much comfort.

To our great relief, Wu was cordial and had everything ready, including the paperwork, which was all in Thai, so Mai Lee looked it over before leaving us to our fate.

I followed Trong down the dock to our junk and we hopped aboard. The boat seemed to smell even worse than before, as if Wu had thrown in more rotten fish, or even a couple of decomposing corpses, at no extra charge. We just held our collective noses.

I inspected the boat to make sure the engine had been replaced, batteries were working, both fuel tanks were full and that all the operating parts looked good to go. Trong fired her up and she sounded like a momma bear coming out of hibernation.

I jumped back on the dock and handed Wu the remaining payment and shook his hand. His Cheshire-cat smile was chilling. I immediately thought of all the ways he could have sabotaged the boat but just nodded and started picking up our gear and tossing it onboard to Trong.

"She all yours. Show biz will be step up for this old fish wife."

"If we can turn her into a thing of beauty, then that'll be real movie magic."

There was no time to waste. We had to have everything fully operational in a hurry so we could motor downriver with the rest of the fleet in the early evening. I couldn't get out of Wu's shipyard fast enough. I handled the engine, pumps and lighting. Trong stowed gear, prepared the sails and inflated the Zodiac. We kept our bag of flashlights, flares and life jackets handy. Funny how much you can get done when you're running on adrenaline. Of course, we did manage to power through all our sandwiches and most of the beer long before we shoved off.

The plodding, stern-mounted rudder took some getting used to. It was controlled by lines and pulleys and I could tell that in high seas and bad weather it would take two of us to turn her.

The engine controls were aged Morse Controls -- one lever for forward and reverse, the other engine speed. Our running lights were operational though they would go dark once we entered the Gulf of Thailand and made our break for open water.

As we maneuvered our way slowly among the other vessels, I just kept praying that we wouldn't hit anything. A junk was a far cry from a Swift Boat in size, weight and agility. Trong moved around the bow to keep watch and guide me out of trouble. Though my preference would have been to find some running room, I had to keep the junk in the middle of the pack without a collision. We got more than a few stares as we came close to other fishermen. It may have been the panicked look on my face that gave them cause to keep a wary eye turned in my direction. Surely, they had seen more than a few ridiculous looking white guys behind the helm of yachts they had bought with no idea of how to sail. But steering a stinking junk, well, this could be a first. I had been sweating since first laying eyes on Wu and now I was soaking wet, even as an evening sea breeze brought some relief to what had been a sweltering, exhausting day.

As we reached the mouth of the river and headed for open water, I remained with the pack until complete darkness allowed me to drift away, extinguish my running lights and begin our course south. There was no moon out yet, and when and if it did appear, it would just be the sliver of a new moon. Magic would be proud of our disappearing act. Now for the real magic -- turning this junk into a Trojan horse.

Once clear of the fishing fleet and certain that no boats were following us, we used my handheld Garmin GPS to chart our course to the west side of Koh Phangan and then to the small islands around Koh Phaluai. En route, we would find a secluded piece of the world to rendezvous with *Freedom*. One of the first things I did was hoist the red flag I'd brought with me. If junk lore was true, red flags kept the dragon happy and warded off typhoons and other bad things. Right now, I was a believer in red flags. I also believed in showers and rigged us up a saltwater version, which was heavenly.

We thought we had enough water and food for three days but realized that we had miscalculated and became extremely careful with the last of everything. On the third night after our departure, we found a remote place to drop anchor and made final radio contact with *Freedom* sending exact coordinates in our pre-established code just to be safe.

Once *Freedom* pulled alongside, we attached stern and bow lines and hoped all the fenders would keep scraping damage to a minimum. Luckily, the seas were calm and the night was cool.

It was good to see Mai Lee, Benny and Chien, who had slipped aboard F*reedom* at the last minute to avoid any notice when the yacht departed. He would be transferring to the junk to help with the conversion. They had already started bringing equipment topside and were ready for us. For four hours, we manhandled gear aboard the junk. Even petite Mai Lee worked like a stevedore. Trong had prepared the junk to accommodate the equipment in a manner that would ensure access to needed items without having to constantly reorganize – food, water, tools, generator, raw materials, specialized equipment, dive gear -- everything had its place. He knew his stuff.

It was 0400 before we finished. Mai Lee and Benny cast off the lines from the junk, turned *Freedom* north and waved good-bye. They would take turns sleeping and would wait until daylight to wash the dirt and grime from *Freedom's* starboard side.

We covered what equipment was on deck with grimy sails, started the engine, pulled up anchor and continued our voyage to Koh Phaluai and its family of islands -- and what a beautiful family it was. Clear turquoise water rushed up to white beaches edged in mangrove forests where hundreds of fish species found hospitable breeding grounds. Palm and coconut trees poked upward from the lush vegetation. We avoided any island with signs of life and finally settled on one with a protective cove where we anchored and got down to business – dirty, hot, sweaty business.

Chapter Nineteen

Trong, Chien and I made a rough layout of the junk and then started developing plans for the moon pool and placement of key equipment. The 2000-year-old basic junk design had not changed much over the centuries, even in our version, a smaller coastal fishing vessel. The sails were lateen, or triangularly shaped, set on long yardarms and mounted at an angle on the mast. The larger mainsail was roughly located at midships. Its mast was mounted through the deck and stepped on the keel. Forward was a smaller foremast. Aft of the mainmast was a mizzen mast whose sail helped trim the helm, mitigating the constant fighting with the helm in bad weather -- simple, but effective.

All the sails had horizontal battens for shape and strength. The individual battens could be trimmed, reefed and adjusted for fullness. We had some sail tears between battens but most were in surprisingly good shape, at least good enough for our purposes.

The four areas of the junk were divided by three watertight bulkheads that ran from the keel to the deck. The two middle holds were accessed by deck hatches, which were four-feet square and elevated above the deck to keep high seas and rain out, protecting the cargo from ruin and the ship from sinking. The area forward of the two center holds was the smallest, its lower section used for net storage and the upper area for crew. The area aft was three decks high, starting with the engine room at the bottom with the midsection designed for fuel and water storage. The upper area, which rose from the main deck to a higher deck was built to house the steering tiller, a galley and the captain's quarters, where we put our sleeping mattresses once we checked for rats. The few we found were all dead. It was not comforting to know that rats had found so promising little onboard that they had abandoned ship. When we did sleep, it was in exhausted stupors, always in shifts with someone standing watch. The evening breeze rescued us from the heat and the star-spangled sky provided all the glitzy entertainment we could want.

Armed with a semblance of a master plan, we first designed the moon pool, fabricating the support frames to carry the load once we penetrated the hull. Next we covered the fabricated area with foam and fiberglass to make it appear as if this part of the hull was damaged. With compartmentalized flooding, we could conceal the actual moon pool without sinking the ship – at least that was the plan – more movie magic.

Next we rigged the dive compressor, the storage bottles and dive equipment. For this, we designed a false bulkhead between the two holds used for fish. We only needed a depth of two feet. Even if both hatch covers were opened at the same time, the false bulkhead would remain undetectable.

The radio was easy to hide but I wasn't sure about how to conceal the extra antenna we'd need. We finally decided to mount a wire antenna in plain view and attach it to a cheap portable radio. Then, when we needed it, we would use jumper cables that could be quickly disconnected.

The eight-year-old generator we lugged onboard looked much too new for the junk so we aged it as much as possible without harming it. Once we had the generator up and running, we set up the dive compressor and storage air bottles against the false fish-hold bulkhead. To bring outside air in for the compressor, we had to cut holes in the hull – additional damage that didn't look at all out of place.

On the port side of the same area, I mounted the water-making equipment. Magic and I had spent a lot of time talking about this. Diving, especially in the tropics, was dehydrating work. We would need a reliable source of good water. Since the reverse-osmosis units worked extremely well, we had bought the necessary components and now mounted them next to the compressor. With a high-pressure pump and two UV filters, we would have access to 100 gallons of fresh water a day – more than enough for all our needs, including a good cup of morning coffee.

I had to keep reminding myself that all of this would be at the bottom of the ocean within weeks, so a long-term preventive maintenance program was not an issue.

While Chien fabricated the fake bulkhead, Trong and I started building the moon pool. We reinforced the pool with enough support that it would not become a huge gaping hole we'd have no control over. Next, we added flotsam -- pieces of jagged wood, fishnet, old lines -- to simulate extensive damage. All this was readily available onboard. Our junk was already a floating wreck before we started making it look worse.

Now Trong and I were ready to put the bilge pump to work. Armed with our damage-control kit, consisting of wooden plugs, canvas and pneumatic drills, we stepped back a moment, took a deep breath and drilled a one-inch hole through the hull, causing a geyser of warm saltwater. The aft hold started to fill and fill and fill. I started to worry when the water reached two feet and damn near panicked when it hit three. It was then that the water flow slowed, finally topping out at approximately three-and-a-half feet. From this hold, we ran to check the entire vessel -- engine room, shaft alley, fishing holds. Miraculously we found only minor seepage, nothing of consequence that would sink us. I continued to be amazed at how well these junks were designed and built. The flotsam floating in the flooded area did indeed give the illusion of severe damage.

After four hours of marking the water level and finding no further flooding, we plugged our test hole and pumped out the water. We were ready. It was time to call Magic.

It was amazing how therapeutic plain old hard work could be. I was hot, grimy, tired and looked like crap, but I was feeling better than I had in a long time. I hoped it would last, that I could take all this energy and focus back to my island home.

Since we had prearranged the following night as our pick-up time with Mai Lee, we were relieved to be running ahead of schedule. Our last job was to take the small stash of weapons we now had onboard and hide them around the junk where they would be readily accessible but not found by prying eyes. Trong had also procured some C4 in case we had to scuttle in a hurry. It was oddly comforting to have this, though we hoped to just ease the junk away from the coral reef and flood all her compartments.

When *Freedom* pulled alongside, we topped off the junk's fuel tanks and brought onboard more food, ice and, most importantly, beer before I jumped ship leaving the junk in the capable hands of Trong and Chien. It was good to be back onboard *Freedom*, where I experienced a renewed appreciation for air-conditioning and refrigeration.

I called Magic that night. He sounded tired but excited that things had gone so smoothly. I gave him a list of the few items we still needed. He thought he could be there within the week and would confirm everything in a couple of days. My job was to check the weather and make sure *Freedom* was ready to go out again.

I turned the phone over to Mai Lee and went into the galley for some water. When I returned to the salon, Mai Lee was off the phone. I sat across from her and looked into her worried face.

"What's wrong, Mai Lee?"

"Uncle Beau, I think Magic is not doing well."

"Mai Lee, Magic and I are getting older. We don't have the energy we once had."

"No, I think it's not age. I'm afraid there's something very wrong with Magic." She started to cry. "I don't want him to make himself sick over the treasure. Benny and I want him, not treasure. Please make him listen. He'll listen to you. We need you to take care of Bac Magic."

"Of course, I'll take care of Magic. That's why I'm here. But talking some sense into him, that's another matter entirely." I took her hand across the table and patted it with more reassurance than I felt. "We're going to do this thing. The treasure is for you but the mission is for Magic -- something he has to do. And I'm the designated event planner and my events are always pulled off at the last moment in spectacular fashion."

"Then you're a magician too."

"I think Magic and I have at least one last trick left in us. You just have to believe."

Chapter Twenty

"What you mean you don't find junk and white guy?" Wu snapped angrily in Chinese, but his Thai crew unhappily understood every word.

Wu was beside himself that the American had disappeared and had done so in his own backyard in a getaway junk he had sold him. His men had easily followed the junk in their motorboat downriver to the Gulf of Thailand. Even in the dark, they had been able to keep track of the tall frame at the helm. But somehow, in open waters, the junk had just disappeared. One moment it was there and the next it was gone. They had searched up and down the coast and even ventured farther out to sea, but nothing. By sunrise, after wandering around in the Gulf, following one junk after another and arguing for hours, they decided they were in enormous trouble. Rather than report back to Wu, they searched for two more days, chasing groups of junks, stealing gasoline when necessary and constantly bickering.

Wu had to be told. Only two of the three dared to face Wu. The deserter would ultimately be hunted down. Wu was relentless. The duo, who decided that they would just as soon die sooner than later, motored back to Wu's shipyard. They would have preferred to swim, anything that would take longer and postpone the wrath of Wu. His mercurial temper and capacity for cruelty made failure a withering option.

Wu paced back and forth in front of his hapless men. He wanted to kill them. He always felt better when he acted on his fury, but decided to give them one more chance because they at least had the guts to face him with bad news. Besides he needed them to relieve his other crew following the woman from the embassy.

"This is your last chance. You lose track of Embassy Girl and you and your families die very slowly."

Relief tempered with renewed fear of failure pulsed through the bodies of the spared crew. The men knew that following the embassy lady was a second chance at life. For the next three weeks, they took turns following Isabella. Her movements became predictable – home to embassy and back with a few errands in the evenings. Her two trips to the yacht club were out of pattern and required more stealth and usually two cars to keep the woman from spotting a tail. It was an unnecessary precaution in light of Isabella's total disregard of even the most basic protocol, which would have involved changing her routes, varying her times and being constantly aware of her surroundings. There was a reason she hadn't been selected for field work – no instincts.

Surveillance was tedious, boring work but Wu's men had many compelling reasons to stay vigilant. Toward the end of the first week, the woman reappeared from her apartment around 7 pm. This was unusual; she didn't seem to have much of a social life. Driving straight to the

Mandarin Oriental Hotel, she left her car with the valet, and in an elegant long emerald gown, strode through the hotel lobby as if she owned the place.

Wu's men split up. One decided to self-park because the car contained weapons. The other followed Embassy Girl into the hotel where he did not exactly blend in with all the finely dressed and coifed people in the lobby who were on their way to the Royal Ballroom for a grand embassy gala. It took an invitation to get in the ballroom so Wu's man waited across the hallway keeping the door in sight at all times. He received more than a few stares and felt very out of place. When his partner-in-crime appeared, they took seats nearby and tried to disappear, pretending to be deep in conversation.

Chapter Twenty-One

Magic's plane was late, so it was almost midnight by the time we checked into the Mandarin Oriental. The grand two-story glass lobby was filled with people. Magic already had a reservation, insisting this was his treat for all my hard work. I certainly wasn't going to decline an opportunity to stay in one of the most historic hotels in Thailand. And she definitely was a grand dame -- elegant, alive with history and intrigue, showing none of her 100-plus years.

It was obvious that there was some major event going on in one of the ballrooms. Shouldering our luggage, we navigated our way through the tuxedos and gowns toward the elevator. One particularly stunning woman in an emerald green strapless dress seemed to take a special interest in us. At first I was sure she wasn't staring at me, then I was flattered and finally unnerved. It had been too long. She seemed embarrassed when I stared back and quickly disappeared in the crowd.

"You've still got it," Magic teased me.

"Yea, the sight of me sends 'em running in the opposite direction."

"She was already attracting some attention from a couple of unsavory characters behind her," Magic whispered under his breath.

I looked where Magic indicated and didn't see the two men he saw. It was obvious that Magic was the one who still had it, who could size up a room or a situation in a moment and see what was out of place.

When we got to our luxury two-bedroom suite with its sweeping river views, I was ready to just collapse on the terrace and stare at the full moon on the river. I knew Magic was beat after the brutally long flight. He looked tired, clammy and even thinner than before, but he perked up when room service arrived with steaks and wine. We both turned in early and started the next morning with breakfast served on the veranda. Wisely, Magic had booked the room for two nights. He needed a chance to get his strength back and we both had lots to discuss – much more than I knew.

From the moment I picked him up, he'd been asking about Mai Lee and Benny and what I thought of them.

"So I see they stole your heart too," he smiled.

"Yep, if Helen were still alive, we'd spirit them away, right from under your wings, and move them to the island. You could visit, of course. Funny how things work out, you and I both childless when you know we'd have made the best fathers ever."

"Maybe that's why this is so important to me. As a SEAL, I could never offer a family much – always gone, forever assignments in some hellhole, never home for dinner."

"Helen and I wanted kids but all those Agent Orange stories were daunting. I didn't want to bring a child into the world just to endure a life of miserable suffering. We've all seen enough of that."

Magic walked out on the terrace and stared down at the river teaming with vessels fringed by a city flaunting itself -- loud, bustling and brightly colored. When he came back into the room, he clearly had something on his mind.

"I really appreciate all you've already done," Magic said as he poured himself a second cup of coffee and sat down across from me. "But I'm going to be asking for more, even more than we originally discussed. Please feel free to say no because it's a lot to expect."

"I'm feeling up for just about anything after the last few weeks, so ask away," I boldly chirped.

"Our diving for teacups could end badly so I'm giving you everything you'll need to have in case anything happens to me. You remember the way we wrote letters home right before some mission from hell?"

I nodded but I didn't want to remember. The dread of going back into Vietnamese waters suddenly washed over me.

"Here are the names and numbers of my attorney and my friend in Immigration. The attorney has access to my apartment, bank accounts, investments, safety deposit box and my will with you named as executor. I've already sold the *Empress* and deposited the funds. What I'm hoping is that you use what I have and whatever my share is from the teacups to help Mai Lee and Bennie get into the States and into college. I've already secured their passports and student visas. I've done all I can but I need to know you can take it from here if I'm not around."

"And here I thought you brought me along just for my charm and good looks," I joked because what Magic was saying was too much to comprehend. I was desperately trying to lighten the situation.

"I don't want you to think I lack the conviction that we can pull this off. I just want a fallback plan," Magic backpedaled, sensing my discomfort.

"This is YOUR dream for these kids. They'd rather have you than any stinkin' treasure and they've made that very clear to me."

"Well, I guess all we can do is try to have it all, but just in case, can I count on you for one last gigantic favor?"

"I'll do my best for them as long as you do your best not to die on me," I finally agreed after a long pause.

"I would feel better knowing I was still around to keep your sorry ass in shape."

"Well, you should be happy now. Thanks to you, I've worked myself into a shocking level of fitness, especially for me. No one's going to know me."

It was done. We had looked into the abyss together and now scampered back to enjoy our friendship and plan one last cockamamie mission.

I was relieved to be able to talk about the mission, something I could actually control to some degree. It was good to relate to Magic that the plan was looking workable, that the junk now passed muster -- so much so it was going to be a shame to sink her. She had been poorly maintained but built well. The junk could be partially flooded and the flooding would hide our alterations and fake compartments. The hole in the bottom of the hull looked real and would be real soon enough. The authorities should be satisfied unless they needed extra convincing with a bribe. But with all this, we still had to find the treasure. If treasure-hunting was like combat, 50% preparation and 50% luck, we were halfway there.

When we left the room to explore the hotel, Magic asked the concierge for a notary and he sat me down to show ID and sign a mountain of paperwork so I'd have access to everything that belonged to Magic and could get to it in a hurry. Once done, everything went to a FedEx agent and from there to Magic's San Diego attorney. For some reason, I felt emotionally drained after the signing ceremony but Magic seemed more energetic, as if he had lightened his load. That in itself was worth a lot to me.

Over lunch of chili prawns and Singha beer, I told Magic he was officially up to speed on what had been done and what lay ahead, at least all I could foresee, which would prove to be woefully inadequate.

We hung out in the hotel and watched for anyone else interested in our presence. I didn't want to run into Wu or his crew by venturing into town. When it was time to go just before dawn, we left the bill on the card, the keys in the room, slipped out the back way, jumped in the Rover and sped through the already waking city in a dizzying series of turns meant to leave pursuers in the dust.

Chapter Twenty-Two

Isabella had been stunned when she sighted Beau with his tall, black, Asian- looking friend in the hotel lobby. She realized that she hadn't been exactly discreet but hoped that Beau believed she was just flirting with him. He had changed since she'd seen him with Wu at the shipyard. The American was tanner, leaner and happier, she thought. It took a moment but she figured his pal must be the owner of *Freedom*. He certainly fit the bartender's basic description.

More pieces kept being added to her puzzle but she still had no idea how they fit together. Nothing made sense. The yacht had vanished for several days but she thought it might be back in port, something that needed to be checked. She hadn't figured out how Wu had anything in common with the American, his friend or the young woman she had seen, unless it was an illegal enterprise – drugs, human trafficking, gun-running. She thought back to the two men in the lobby. They were obviously friends, both with a definite military bearing. Perhaps they were mercenaries, or weapons buyers, or both. This scenario took root in her brain and grew like a weed with no help from facts or any other sustaining elements.

Isabella paced around her office. She was finding it much too confining for her career aspirations. Translating one more inconsequential document was going to send her over the edge. She wanted to do more digging and decided that Bert, her IT friend downstairs, would be most helpful if she were her usual charming self.

Within 15 minutes of entering Bert's office, Isabella had the name of Beau's friend. He was James Black, an American, who had recently visited Bangkok on several occasions. If she wanted to know more, she'd need to ask Bert out, preferably before he was caught for hacking into the classified files Isabella had asked to see.

After work, Isabella went home, changed and headed for the yacht club. As usual, she had no clue that she had a tail, even though Wu's men were not particularly adept at their jobs. They had, however, seen enough in the lobby of the Mandarin Oriental to make a report to Wu of a sighting of the junk buyer with a tall, dark man. They didn't understand exactly how what they'd seen would matter to Wu, but he seemed sufficiently pleased to ensure that they would live longer, happier lives.

Chapter Twenty-Three

Once Magic was sighted headed for *Freedom*, Mai Lee and Benny rushed out to greet him. It was a hero's welcome. He was visibly touched.

"Let's see what you two have been up to while I've been gone. Beau tells me you have somehow made him look good."

"We missed you," Mai Lee exclaimed as she hugged Magic for a long time. Benny and Magic exchanged bear hugs and big grins.

Magic did indeed have his little family. I stood back savoring the moment. Magic reached around and motioned me to join the gathering, and for the first time in a long time, I felt as if I belonged somewhere.

We huddled around the table in the salon and went over maps, charts and our master checklist.

Well, I think we're ready," said Magic slowly as Mai Lee spread a lunch of cold crayfish and salad across the table. "We'll leave later tonight. We need enough gas for the junk and the Zodiac and extra oil. The Zodiac gives us a getaway vehicle, if we need one, and a way to ferry ourselves and the treasure back to *Freedom* when the time comes. What a glorious time that will be."

Cheers went up around the table and we all spontaneously placed our hands, one on top of the other, and let out a convincing "Hooyah."

"Now let's see what we have in the way of firepower," Magic suggested, moving right along.

Benny pulled out the weapons cache which we had already raided for the junk. Magic left two 12-gauge shotguns, two Winchester Model 1300 Defenders and one 9-mm Browning Hi-Power with extra magazines for *Freedom* and put both Ruger mini-14s aside for the junk. Onboard the junk, we already had one shotgun, a couple of handguns and now the two Ruger semi-automatic rifles.

"And we come in peace," laughed Magic as he assessed our weaponry. "I think I can now take a nap with complete peace of mind. We should all get some rest. Wake me when we're ready to shove off." He kissed us all on the top of the head and pointed himself toward the master stateroom.

I reassured myself that Mai Lee and Benny knew how to handle the weapons they had and then went over the checklist one last time before I headed topside for a walk in the sultry air. I wouldn't be on terra firma for a while and I wanted that connection -- feet on the ground. The slips around *Freedom* were empty and there was only one yacht coming in past the long U-shaped wave-breaker. People came and went from the yacht club hotel and somewhere some 60s rock was playing -- Otis Redding's *Dock of the Bay*.

When I first heard that song in 1969, the dock I was on wasn't attached to a yacht club overlooking a shimmering sea; it was a dock composed of barges, named Sea Float, a primitive ops base out of which I ran patrols along the Mekong River and its tributaries, canals and oversized ditches. My waterway back then was the muddy silt run-off leavings of one of the world's mightiest and longest rivers. It came to life somewhere in the Tibetan Plateau and coursed through China, Burma, Laos, Thailand, Cambodia and, finally, came to an ignominious end in Vietnam. The silt was so thick it looked and felt like mud, choking the awaiting open waters of the Gulf of Thailand for miles out. If I ever had to jump in the muddy river or any of its tributaries, once back in the boat I quickly dried into a fearsome-looking dirtball.

I still remembered the smell of the Mekong -- more that of a plowed field than the fresh-water woodsy rivers and streams I knew from home. These had power over me from an early age. I wanted to know all their mysteries. When I first saw the Atlantic Ocean, I toddled toward it at such speed that my dad beat all previously held sprint records, or at least that's how he told the story. So much of my life had taken place on the water – many of the best things like meeting Helen on a dive and the worst in running the Mekong. And now this treasure hunt in waters far from home and too close to my past. I walked along the beach until I wore myself out in the heat and then headed back to *Freedom*.

Everyone had crashed except for Mai Lee who was busy cooking in the galley. She gave me a little worried smile and I gave her a reassuring hug. It was late when we gathered round the table for supper and it was dark when we raised the mainsail and eased out of our slip. We were bound for whatever glory we might find in diving for teacups and their tiny capacity to serve up a taste of redemption. It was blessedly quiet – one lone boat under sail on calm seas. No activity within sight or on the radar and our good weather was supposed to hold for at least the next week. A half moon appeared amid a sky quickly turning on all its heavenly lights as the sweetness of frangipani rode the onshore breeze with provocative promise.

Chapter Twenty-Four

It was a long sail back to the junk, about 240 nautical miles. Even with *Freedom* sailing along at seven to ten knots, almost twice the junk's best, we had some time to relax and joke around. Mai Lee thought the junk should have a name, which initiated a round of laughter and a litany of derisive monikers. It turned out she was serious, and after more hooting, we got serious too and gave the junk her nom de treasure -- *Discovery* or *Khám Phá* in Vietnamese. So now our home for the next few weeks would have a sobriquet to make it seem more like a real place to live rather than the filthy, stinkin' deathtrap it actually was. Later, we would break a beer bottle over her bow and make it official.

Magic seemed like his old self, as if the sea air really did have the marvelous recuperative powers ascribed to it for centuries. He spent lots of time with Mai Lee and Benny, talking about what they wanted to study, what they wanted to do in life. Mai Lee asked about her father, a father she couldn't really remember, and Magic served up some good stories about the times they fought, laughed and drank together.

As we approached the rendezvous point with *Discovery*, we radioed ahead, got the all-clear sign from Chien and Trong and proceeded to close the distance and pull alongside. Once we were securely tied up, there was an exchange of hugs and smiles and the refueling and re-provisioning began. When everything was done, there were beers all around and I went below decks on *Freedom* and dug out my 35-mm Nikon and took it topside for photos. Magic seemed particularly pleased to see me capturing this moment and getting everyone in the picture with both candid and posed shots. It was the first time since Helen's death that I'd gotten back into my photography. I got lots of pictures of the kids with Magic, and Mai Lee insisted on a picture of Magic and me. At one point, I turned on the timer and stood with the others for the all important commemorative group photo. The dawn was just breaking and the light was good. With so much already done and so much possibility ahead, spirits were high.

When it was time for us go our separate ways – the *Discovery* to the treasure and *Freedom* back to the yacht club – Benny promised Magic he'd take good care of Mai Lee and I promised Mai Lee I'd take good care of Magic. We all knew that the reverse could happen. Trong and Chien would be our fishermen if we were boarded. Trong had the experience to deal with the authorities and Chien had a sweet charm that just might pass for a young boy learning the ropes from his fisherman father, or whatever story we concocted. Magic and I would assume our positions in the moon pool should there be a boat inspection, but we could get out if matters escalated. We had rigged a way to hear deck conversations and both Trong and Chien knew to use the distress word if they were in trouble.

We waved at Mai Lee and Benny until they were out of sight and then made preparations to set sail. Once we weighed anchor, we set our course for Hon Tay Island and teacup treasure. We would rely only on the sails when the winds were strong, and when there was little wind and we were under power, the sails would add speed and fuel efficiency. Our junk *Discovery* was almost beautiful under full sail. The design was ancient and our boat had been seriously neglected, but the lateen sails were a wonder to behold.

When we had gotten underway, Magic handed me a sheaf of papers he took from a leather pouch. He motioned for Trong to join us.

"This is what you'll need for the Vietnamese authorities," he explained. "Put them in a safe, dry place that you can get to quickly."

Everything was in Vietnamese so I handed the bundle to Trong. He looked through the papers, smiled and put them in a watertight cabinet under the chart table.

"So where did you get those?" I asked bemused.

"Once a black ops guy, always a black ops guy," he smiled and relieved Chien at the helm.

When it was my turn to relieve Magic, I noticed his dark expression.

"Aside from the sheer overwhelming nature of this operation, what's got you so worried?"

"We're at least a man short. There should be a big, ugly SEAL warrior onboard *Freedom*. Those kids are good but they're still just kids. I won't rest easy until we're all back together."

"Yea, it worries me too. Trong would have been perfect to go with them but we need him here. Once they're safely back at the yacht club, they'll call us on the single sideband. Then the next call will be from us for a rendezvous. And you know they'll call if there's trouble."

"I can't stand to see them in more danger. What if I get them killed with my crazy-ass plan?" Magic was genuinely worried and looked even feverish in his anxiety.

"The faster we get in and get out, the better."

"May the teacup gods smile on us."

Magic sighed and turned in for a while. We rotated through four-hour watches. There were always two of us on deck scanning the horizon and hoping not to see anything. Our route from Koh Phaluai toward Phu Quoc, approximately 300 nautical miles, would have us coming up from the south, not the west because we wanted to appear as if we'd been blown off course from the eastern side of Vietnam.

The junk averaged four-to-six knots, approximately 100 nautical miles a day. At this rate, we would be in Vietnamese waters in three days. We needed to reach the treasure site with the afternoon sun. That would put the sun behind us as we approached the reef near Hon Tay Island. Only with the sun behind us would we be able to see the reef underwater as we approached. From any other position, the sun's glare would make seeing the reef impossible. We had come too far to miss the damn thing; or worse yet, crash into it.

On the second day, Magic and I donned loose-fitting, cool black pajamas and conical straw hats, a native garb we hoped would make us look as if we belonged on a Vietnamese fishing boat, at least from a distance. They were the same type of pajamas worn by NVA commandos during the war and we took their fighting ability seriously – pajamas or no pajamas. I never thought the day would come when Magic Man and I would be wearing the preferred garb of our onetime enemy.

A fairly steady breeze filled our sails and made life on the junk tolerable. The cooler the breeze, the less everything smelled and the better we slept. Daily squalls portended the monsoon season's full-blown arrival. We were counting on the monsoons to camouflage our treasure hunt. Rain wouldn't interfere with the diving but it would reduce and possibly eliminate aerial reconnaissance. We hoped it would also limit surface patrols, especially in such a remote part of the country. The Vietnamese had metal patrol boats and some wooden ones called Yabuta junks. If we'd had radar on the junk, we could have picked up the metal ones but the wooden boats, like our junk, would not show up on the screen.

The water-maker worked like a charm and we went through a lot of it. During heavy monsoons, we wouldn't really need one if we had a good capture system. However, just the thought of collecting water off the junk's decks was enough to send me to the nearest infirmary -- except there wasn't one, though we did have a fairly extensive first-aid kit.

Later that day, we got the all-safe call from Mai Lee and Benny. I heard Magic warn them to be careful even in the marina. Before he signed off, he handed me the headset so I could hear their voices, which were striking a cheery tone meant to mask underlying worry. Magic and I were both relieved to hear from them. We lavished on the reassurances and promised to call soon.

They were two incredible kids. When the three of us had time together sailing back from the junk to pick up Magic, we had gotten better acquainted. They had wanted to know about Helen. I realized that as I talked about her for the first time that I started to feel better, as if I were keeping her alive through my stories. Mai Lee and Benny bombarded me with questions about our life together and where we lived – if it was like Vietnam or Thailand.

I began by telling them about Helen's first trip to my home along the Carolina coast. We visited Nags Head, Hatteras and Oracoke Island. She fell in love with the deserted beaches and the food – she-crab soup, fried oysters and hush puppies. I was both her tour guide and interpreter, since she couldn't understand a word of the brogue, which was near-perfect Elizabethan English.

As we headed south from Ocracoke to the Cedar Island Ferry, she looked at me with a big smile and, in her best Southern accent, declared, "I could live here; this is heaven."

That night we stayed in the small hamlet of Sea Level on the Core Sound. Over beer, fresh oysters and steamed, spicy blue crabs, Helen insisted on knowing everything she could about my part of the world. In particular the history and the legends, such as the stories about Blackbeard and how he once blockaded the port of Charleston and held its citizens hostage until a ransom was paid. He was killed in battle but his fearsome image lived on along the coast, though he supposedly never harmed his captives.

As I retold the story to Mai Lee and Benny, they were just as excited as Helen had been, which made me happy.

The wild horses of the Outer Banks enthralled Helen and I now found a new audience as I recounted how these gorgeous creatures still roamed free in the Northern Outer Banks along Corolla, where they were first sighted in the 1500s -- believed to be Spanish Mustangs that had survived a shipwreck.

I didn't know how I could top this story for the kids but their attention wasn't waning, so over lunch I recounted how I had driven Helen up the back roads on Bogue Inlet, where we enjoyed a picnic across the water from a primeval island, connected to Bogue by an old wooden bridge.

When an elderly black gentleman approached us, we exchanged greetings and he joined us for a cold beer. For an hour, we enjoyed his company and his colorful, affectionate descriptions of all that had transpired on this coastline.

I asked him if any of the islands were for sale. He answered with a question.

"You in that war zone?"

"Vietnam?" I questioned.

"Yes, sar," he looked at me steadily.

"Yes, sir, I was."

"I thought so," he said. "I kin see it in your eyes. Just a little though. This lady bringin' back the light."

"I believe you're right," I agreed. "I'm a mighty lucky man."

"You 'bout 29?"

"Yes, sir, I'm 28."

"That's how old my boy woulda been if he'd come home."

Tears came to Helen's eyes and she reached over and hugged him. "Your boy and my brother," she confided.

We sat for a bit, silent and sad, but comforted by the company of one another.

This was how Helen and I first met John Luke Whitaker and his wife Beulah. Late in the 1800s, his family had come north from the South Carolina Low Country and he still retained some of his Gullah accent. Over the first of many fine meals, we sat at the Whitaker's table and got to know them. Their son had been a Marine in I Corps. He had survived two tours, including Khe Sanh, only to be killed in a helo crash three weeks before coming home.

Their other three children, all girls, were married and spread over North Carolina. One was a doctor, the other two teachers. They were understandably proud of their girls and their son, but were still haunted by his loss.

The next day we stopped by the Whitakers to say good-bye. I had seven more days of leave before I had to report back to San Diego. For some reason, Helen and I just didn't want to leave. We sat drinking lemonade with John and Beulah on their front porch. We had agreed on first names, even though I was always more comfortable calling my elders by title and surname.

"What you all want to buy land for, Beau?"

"We want to live here, John," I answered looking him straight in the eye.

"You all want to live here?" Beulah asked.

"Yes, ma'am," replied Helen, quickly catching on to Southern mannerisms.

"Why?"

I thought for a moment. "I don't know exactly -- mostly because it's home."

The Whitakers exchanged a look and a nod before John said, "Come with us."

The four of us walked down the road to where we had first met John. He led us over the wooden bridge to the island we had spotted while picnicking. The tour of the 10-acre paradise revealed lush trees, plants, blue heron, an osprey and dozens of skittering critters, as well as an oyster bed and a creek that ran right down the middle of the island.

Helen couldn't contain herself. "Oh, Beulah, it's beautiful. What a Garden of Eden!"

As we retraced our steps over the bridge, we kept turning back for one last glimpse.

"Thank you both for showing us this hidden paradise. What a wonderful island! If we can find any place half as wonderful as this, we're moving back here as soon as I'm out of the Navy – that is if Helen feels the same way I do."

"Absolutely," Helen chimed in.

John stopped and looked at his wife.

"Beulah?"

"I think so, John."

They looked at us and John said simply, "Well, I think we'd like you to move here."

"Excuse me?" I responded.

"That there is our land," said John. "If you want to move in, we'd like to have you as neighbors."

Both Benny and Mai Lee thought this was a great story. They had never really thought about how the war affected so many others so far away. With their fingers, they traced the distance on our map from Vietnam to the States and found North Carolina and, finally, the Outer Banks, my home. They were still looking for a place to call home and hoped to see my home someday. I could just envision Helen welcoming these kids into our house, but that picture slipped away as the sound of a circling aircraft disrupted my reverie.

Chapter Twenty-Five

Magic gave us a "look alive" warning just as the plane came in for a closer look. We were just about to enter Vietnamese waters so this fly-by wasn't unexpected. We had raised a tattered Vietnamese flag and had spread fish nets everywhere. Surely we passed as working fishermen from above. The pilot soon lost interest as we prepared for much more scrutiny once inside Vietnamese waters. We sorely missed *Freedom's* 48-nautical-mile Furuno radar, with its transducer high in the mast, providing a visual on possible bogeys in the waters south of Phu Quoc Island. The original plan had kept *Freedom* close by in international waters, but Magic had abandoned this idea thinking it would put the kids in too much danger. *Freedom* had been seen near the treasure site only a few months before and was the kind of yacht people remembered.

The day had been spent making the junk look like a functioning fishing boat while hiding anything that might give away our mission. We prepared our moon pool hideaway for quick entry should we be boarded. We crossed into Vietnamese waters shortly before noon, estimating our anchorage in three hours, just the right time to have the best visibility of the reef.

Magic, Trong and Chien all seemed calm, but I was nervous as hell. It had been a long time since I had been near these waters and facing this kind of danger. I wanted off the boat. I wanted to go home. What had seemed reasonable on paper now seemed like total madness – stupidity on steroids. I almost jumped out of my skin when Magic patted me on the shoulder.

"Been a while, hasn't it, Beau?"

"Not long enough, Magic. You and I swore we'd never come back here if we made it out alive."

"We're not going in-country. We're just here to find one particular coral reef and pick up a few teacups. This is nothing compared to what we've seen."

What Magic said made logical sense, but I was running off an overloaded memory bank that triggered every primitive flight-or-fight response I had in me.

"You will make sure we're not killed or captured over tea," I threw back at Magic.

"That was my promise," he confirmed, patting my shoulder and turning his attention to checking the weapons one last time before putting them away.

I took deep breaths and concentrated my mind on giving the junk another once-over to make sure we hadn't missed anything. It wasn't long before we could see Phu Quoc Island in the distance. With surprisingly little effort, I started living our cover. We were the hapless crew of a poor fishing junk blown off course and now headed toward Vietnam's largest island, a palm-tree covered tropical oasis with quaint thatch-roofed homes and harbors dotted with brightly colored fishing boats, overshadowed more and more by relentless development. It was hard to believe that this island haven was only an hour's flight from Ho Chi Minh City -- or as we knew it a lifetime ago -- Saigon.

As Vietnam experienced one war after another, Phu Quoc remained almost untouched. It was off-limits to foreigners and was a place of exile, where prisoners were kept by the French and later by the South Vietnamese, until the end of the Vietnam War in 1975. After the war, people came to live, fish and cultivate pepper. It wasn't too long before the tourists trickled in. It would soon be discovered to the point that what it had been could no longer be found – the sleepy villages crushed by high-rise hotels and busloads of tourists – Vietnam's version of Phuket.

What I remembered most about Phu Quoc, besides its hot, humid monsoonal sub-equatorial climate, was its nuoc mam. This highly acclaimed fish sauce, derived from anchovies caught right offshore, saved many a C-ration-dulled palate, mine included.

There would be no nuoc mam this trip. We threaded our way around the archipelago of 26 islands surrounding Phu Quoc and tightened our course for the isolated reef west of Hon Tay Island.

When we were close, approaching the reef to our starboard, we dropped sail and motored the final mile to our anchorage. Trong was at the helm and I climbed the foremast to guide us in. The water was flat, calm and crystal clear. As we approached the reef, it looked dangerously close to the surface. I called for emergency reverse and we came to a stop. The reversing of the propeller caused ripples on the ocean surface and gave me a truer idea of the depth – approximately five fathoms I reckoned. Chien confirmed this with the depth finder.

"Trong, come ahead slowly." I called out.

We dropped anchor just next to the sand bowl in the middle of the reef. I slipped into the warm water to check the anchor. Everything seemed secure. We shut down the engine and were greeted by jungle noises from the small island just off our anchorage.

There was no other boat on the horizon and no planes overhead. Big thunderheads loomed on the horizon. Bad weather would be our friend as long as it didn't get too crazy. Magic, Trong and I headed below decks to start working on flooding the moon pool and enlarging our test hole in the hull to the size suitable for a diver. Chien took the first watch and kept checking the horizon with binoculars. Trong was a good father to Chien, teaching the boy everything he knew and turning him into a first-rate sailor, scholar and soldier.

As I drilled and sawed through the hull within the reinforced struts we'd added to keep the whole from tearing open, Trong readied the bilge pump. Magic was busy pulling out the dive gear and filling the tanks. It was obvious he wanted to get in one dive right away. We had the lamps and flares to dive round the clock. All four of us were experienced divers but Trong and Chien would be needed on deck most of the time, so Magic and I would shoulder the underwater duties of the operation.

We all seemed to realize we were on the clock. The longer we stayed, the greater the chance of being boarded. And the longer Mai Lee and Benny were alone, the more Magic and I would worry. We had both made our bones on quick in-and-out ops, so this should be like old times, which was both a comforting and troubling thought.

Chapter Twenty-Six

Isabella had gotten to the yacht club after *Freedom* had sailed. There seemed to be no information about its return but the slip was still reserved. She vowed to keep making regular trips to the yacht club, though she was getting very discouraged. It was highly likely she was on a wild-goose chase, but she left her card with the bartender and asked him to give her a call if he noticed *Freedom* in port. Isabella had promised with a wink to make the call worth his while

Her embassy buddy, Bert, had come through for her and found that both James Black and Beau MacEvoy were highly decorated Navy vets, one a retired admiral. They had no criminal records or ties to mercenary organizations. But they had to be mercenaries – it was the only thing that fit in Isabella's conspiratorial mind. They were no longer able to live on their military pensions and had gone back into the warfare business with folks who paid incredibly well. A lot of little wars around the world were funded by illegal drugs, so that could be the vets' connection to Wu and his junk. Then again, Wu could be easily adding arms-dealing to his long list of criminal activities.

Isabella desperately wanted it to be true. She hungered for her big break in the spy game. She would get to the bottom of all this, even if it killed her.

Meanwhile Isabella's faithful companions kept Wu apprised of all her comings and goings.

They had handled this important assignment for several weeks without one screw-up, which was a record for them. Wu had sent his big, bald lieutenant, Jianjun, back to the hotel to find out more about the junk buyer and his friend. Jianjun had spotted them a couple of times but they were wary and alert and eventually gave him the slip. This made Isabella all the more valuable, even though Wu wasn't at all sure there was a connection between the junk buyer and Embassy Girl. He did, however, have all his sources looking for the junk. He would know if it pulled into any port within a 500-mile radius. Wu still considered the possibility that the American was actually shooting a movie and had just returned to Bangkok to meet with his money man or someone connected with the production. Still something smelled as fishy as the boat Wu had sold the tall white guy.

Expecting some unusually large shipments in the coming weeks, Wu was on high alert. He was certain that no smuggling could be done in Thailand by either Americans or Vietnamese. He knew this market and all the players. Outsiders would receive no assistance in Thailand or from the Shan in Burma. Entrepreneurs were discouraged and territories protected. Wu had grown his power by being ever vigilant, seizing every new opportunity and being utterly ruthless. Wu had no friends but he did have paid informants and collaborators in the police, the military, the government and the business community. He rewarded them handsomely and scared them immensely. Wu eliminated even perceived threats to his fiefdom. He believed Embassy Girl was the weak link in whatever was unfolding, and he would have no trouble getting her to tell him everything. He just wasn't sure she knew that much. The longer he left her free to snoop around, the more likely he might actually learn something that mattered.

Chapter Twenty-Seven

"Moon Pool" was a very romantic name for the jagged hole we created in an already much-abused hull. Any lover of form-follows-function design would have felt miffed at our actions; a lover of wooden sailing vessels would have been appalled. It was a far cry from Captain Nemo's exotic diving mechanism aboard the *Nautilus*, but we weren't planning on making it work for 20,000 leagues, just for the time needed to uncover a few extremely rare teacups.

It took three hours of standing waist-deep in water and sawing underwater until we could get a crowbar to rip the wood, creating the rough edges that would best replicate a collision with a coral reef.

The results were dramatic, beyond our wildest expectations. First and most importantly, we didn't sink. However, this unthinkable fate did appear to be a real possibility for what seemed like a very long time. The reflected light from the sandy bottom showed a gaping hole from a bad accident at sea. It was convincing to me and I knew it was man-made destruction months in the planning.

The moon pool filled with water from the expanded opening and the flow was contained -- high enough to make it look as if the junk was disabled and to obscure what wasn't meant to be seen by unwelcome visitors. This amount of water did the job. Everything held the way it was supposed to and there appeared no threat of sinking *Discovery* until we were ready.

Magic was the first to dive out through the opening and I followed right behind, checking the anchor one more time before catching up to him. The water was warm and clear – visibility to at least 100 feet. Brightly colored fish and coral surrounded us. It was a diver's dream come true. The sand bowl on top of the reef was larger than I remembered. If there was treasure in there, it was going to take a lot of careful digging.

Our plan was to divide and conquer – surveying and partitioning the reef into sections and giving each section a letter. There was actually method to our madness. We started with the section closest to the open ocean. This was where I'd found the cup and where we theorized the ship would have first hit the reef. All cargo, including teacups, would have been carefully packed in crates stored below decks. If the hull was split open, the crates would have fallen out. It was hard to believe that any of the wooden crates or metal boxes would still be intact. It was even harder to believe that we were here in all this water looking for something as small and fragile as priceless teacups.

We started our search in section A using ping-pong paddles to remove the sand, waving the paddle over the sand for hours until we reached a depth of three feet where we encountered mud. Then we moved on to the next section of the grid and repeated the process. It was tedious work but we had lots of colorful distractions – fish of every size and description, most I couldn't name. They were much more curious than afraid.

The waters of the Gulf of Thailand were close to what some call the epicenter of the Indo-Pacific. The great profusion of fish found here lived mostly in shallow areas in and around coral reefs. While there were predators, we were only worried about sea snakes and tiger sharks.

There were dozens of types of sea snakes and most lived in warm tropical waters like the Gulf of Thailand and in the Indian and Pacific Oceans, though they did have a tremendous range. They were a variety of colors, patterns and temperaments. Most were curious, but some came with an attitude and were downright belligerent. A pissed-off sea snake, with venom more deadly than a cobra, was something to worry about.

I had more time than I wanted to observe them as I gently stirred the sand and brought them out of hiding. They had paddle tails and extended stomachs that acted as a keel. Like their desert cousins on land, they used their tongues and tasted and possibly smelled the water in front of them to sense disturbances and contemplate prey.

Tiger sharks cruised the shallows mostly at night and, in this area, they could grow quite large -- 12 to 15 feet was not uncommon. So each time a shadow obscured the sunlight filtering down to us, my heart raced and I readied myself to meet one of these big guys with all the teeth. We carried powerheads and dive knives (good for protection or dining selection) but I would have preferred an underwater bazooka.

Magic and I were running low on air so we headed up toward *Discovery*, pulling ourselves up into the ship through the gaping hole in the hull. The grueling routine had begun. Dive, eat, sleep, dive. And always hydrate.

Chien has mercifully taken on the job of cook and cleaned up the galley to the point that it appeared a relatively safe place to prepare, cook and eat food. He fired up the wood-burning stove and made us delicious rice dishes, some with fresh fish he'd caught from the boat. We had installed a small fridge that ran off the generator and kept perishables and beer cold, though there was no drinking for the divers, not yet anyway. Having a galley made the junk seem a little cozier but no one was getting comfortable. Chien took turns with Trong on watch and Magic and I concentrated on getting as much diving and searching done as humanly possible.

After a week of waving the ping-pong paddle over the sand on our reef, I was familiar with most of the life on the reef. It was like knowing my way around town, only on my northeast corner was a peculiar cleaning station manned by bluestreak cleaner wrasses that would swim out of the coral's protection to clean the dead skin, scales and parasites from large fish. Their main customers appeared to be grouper, but on a number of occasions, I watched hammerhead sharks frequent the station. They would come to a standstill about two feet above the coral allowing the wrasses to swim up and clean away, not just skin but inside those hard-to-reach gills. Before I knew it, I too was a customer. My wetsuit had picked up parasites and the bluestreakers paid me a visit and cleaned me right up, not just my wetsuit but the dead skin on my sunburned ears. Wrasses all started out as females with the strongest female changing to male when a male died off, a sequential hermaphrodite transformation that seemed very efficient if a bit daunting, except for the boldest of metrosexuals. My biggest worry was not the sexuality of the bluestreak cleaners but the blenny that mimicked the wrasses. The blenny disdained parasites and preferred to nibble on healthy skin.

Back in the water first thing every morning for more days than I cared to count, I was busy cleaning quadrants when suddenly my light from above was almost totally obscured. It had looked a little like rain when I went in the water so a storm could be rolling in but no, there was light in other directions. No sharks anywhere. In fact, the water seemed clear of all life.

It was still some moments before I realized exactly what was causing the massive shadow. It was alive but it wasn't a shark. Above our dive spot and just below the water's surface was a huge, writhing ball formed by hundreds of sea snakes, wrapping around one another in endless knots. It was impossible to see where one snake ended and the other began and, frankly, I didn't want to get close enough to find out. But there they were churning between me and my moon-pool hatch.

I had been prepared for many scenarios – sharks, pirates and plain defeat – but swimming through a tangled mass of poisonous sea snakes had not even entered my mind. I tried unsuccessfully to recall what Nick Nolte did in *The Deep* when he was on the bottom of the ocean with sharks circling on the surface. Not only couldn't I remember but I realized this wasn't a movie and I would have preferred sharks. The snakes showed no sign of moving along. In fact, they seemed to have incapacitated themselves from anything but spinning in the water. And the more they spun, the greater the frenzy. They were agitated and my presence would not be welcome. Luckily, for now, they didn't seem to notice me, but if I headed for the boat, they would. I didn't have much air left and absolutely no idea about what to do.

Of course, with Magic around, I never needed to worry. Like some superhero, Magic dived out of the moon pool with a spare air hose, which he used like a garden hose to create a circle of bubbles. After a few seconds, the snakes moved away from the bubbles, creating an escape hole directly under the ship. Magic frantically motioned me up and I used the last of my air to head for the opening. He was using the air storage bottle, letting it flow freely for as long as it had air, which luckily was just long enough to get us both clear of the snake ball and safely in the moon pool.

While the snakes never seemed focused on us, they were obviously aggravated by the air bubbles interrupting their orgy. Some snakes had gotten free of the others and were entering the flooded hole of the junk. We scampered out of the water as we watched most of the snakes swim out of the ship and rejoin their brethren.

"You bit?" asked Magic.

"I don't know for sure, but we'll know very soon, won't we? How about you?"

"No, just scared to death."

"Right," I said, "a Snake-Eater scared of snakes."

But as flippant as I wanted to sound, I soon started to shake.

"Damn, it's cold," I said, trying to get out of my wetsuit as Magic threw me a blanket. I couldn't see any bite marks but I was not consoled. Once bitten by a sea snake, there was usually no pain at first, then stiffness and muscle ache set in about half an hour later, followed by blurred vision, sleepiness and, lastly, respiratory paralysis. Even if I hadn't been bit, I was going to experience all the debilitating symptoms in my head.

Magic got me topside and lying down on my air mattress before he pulled out the first-aid kit, which included snake-bite remedies – none of which would probably work in this case. There seemed to be no visible puncture wound so I gradually got my heart rate and blood pressure under control. An hour later, I started to feel halfway normal again and another life-saving moment found its way into Magic lore – only by the time we'd retold this one a few times, it would be THOUSANDS of snakes.

It had started raining and the snakes were still circling so we decided to get a little rest. Though I was glad to be alive, I was emotionally wrung out. Magic seemed to be running on adrenalin half the time and needed to crash. And all of us sensed that this was going to take more time and effort and deadly encounters than we'd anticipated. It also appeared that the monsoon season was coming in early, and with it came the possibility of typhoons.

Trong took the watch and Chien joined the fitful sleepers. He would relieve Trong in four hours. It was the kind of existence that couldn't be sustained indefinitely. We all knew that.

Magic and I awoke early and hungry. Facing death always worked up an appetite. Chien was cooking and he had our unwavering attention and gratitude. He prepared eggs and ham and we all decided to name him MVP of the morning, a morning which smiled on us with a bright, sunny countenance. No clouds in the sky and no snakes in the water below.

Back to teacup diving and back to believing that we had to find something soon. And we did – a large iron nail attached to some wood. It wasn't treasure but it did lift our spirits and reinforce our waning hope.

From the beginning, we had been fanning away the two-to-three feet of sand in each quadrant until we reached the muddy bottom, thinking that was sufficient. But the nail was found in the mud, barely visible, so we had to go deeper.

The treasure, if there was any, was in the mud. The good news was that it was probably well-preserved. The bad news was that it could take months to uncover anything in the mud, even with a well-equipped salvage ship.

We concentrated our efforts on the quadrant where the nail was found and used entrenching tools to penetrate the mud. The hand shovels worked well enough but the process was slow going. We had a lot of ground to cover unless we got lucky soon.

Chapter Twenty- Eight

As I dug away at the mud, I was disheartened. A major key to a successful mission was bringing the right tools. Magic and I had definitely brought knives to a gunfight. The ground that could be explored in hours in the sand with paddles would take days to get through when we were dealing with mud. It was much harder to see what we were doing and it was much harder to do.

We needed a new plan or at least new methods. I was giving this a lot of thought when Magic came to the rescue – again.

When I surfaced after a two-hour stint of unproductive mud-digging, I was greeted by that big Magic smile. He held out a three-meter length of petrol pipe with an air hose near one end.

"Beau," he trumpeted, "behold the magic wand!"

"I would expect nothing less from you, but what the hell does that thing do? Can we wave it around and find the treasure?"

"Precisely. This is our dredge, our mud-sucker. It'll save your manicure and may get us out of here while we're still young and handsome."

"After that build-up, you will understand my skepticism. How does it work?"

"We inject air by this valve into this end of the pipe," Magic explained. "As it rises up through the pipe, it creates suction, hopefully enough to suck out the mud. The mud exits the pipe behind the diver. I have reduced the size of the intake and we can increase suction and control the airflow with this valve on the air hose. The length of pipe may need adjustment to get the necessary suction, but it's ready for a test run. Are you up to going back in for a demonstration?"

"Hell, yes! This could be just what we need."

I took the magic wand down to my dig. As soon as I opened the valve, the mud started flying but with too much force. It only took a small turn of the valve to create the precise suction necessary to clear the mud. I was elated, as happy as the first cave man who learned how to use the first tool on Earth.

"Magic, you're a genius," I told him, once I surfaced. "It works like a champ and only uses a small amount of air. I think we can find whatever's here in record time."

My prediction came true in less than five hours. Magic found pot shards and bits of fine china. The pots were brown clay and appeared to have been 24 inches tall with an eight-inch opening. They flared out to an 18-inch diameter and then tapered down to an eight-inch base. They had an amphora shape without the handles – plain in appearance but elegant in a simple utilitarian design, more Greek-looking than Chinese and more suited for commoners' use than royalty.

I was happy we were finding something, but I was frustrated by the fact that what we were finding seemed to have nothing in common with our original teacup.

The next day, I uncovered another pot. This time it was intact. Using the wand and trowel, we managed to extract it without damage. We brought it onboard and found it was full of mud. As we cleaned out the mud, we found our first china piece. It was a small porcelain cup, cracked in half. But there was more mud, so we kept cleaning and that's when we found the second cup and it was in one piece and perfect.

We were jumping up and down and laughing and high-fiving and acting as if we'd lost our minds. We didn't care how crazy we looked because we had found the treasure.

The clay pots were merely packing cases for the valuable china. Straw was probably added for extra protection and cushioning. In any case, we now knew that at least two priceless cups had survived the voyage, a typhoon, the final sinking and over 200 years in the ocean.

Magic and I couldn't get back to digging fast enough. We found more pots with more cups, mostly intact, and even a couple of teapots. As the days unfolded, we brought onboard additional cups, glass bottles, galley utensils and a dagger.

Our original treasure storage space was full and we had to find new places to hide the bounty. We had surpassed our dreams of discovery and I was well aware of the consequences of pushing our luck.

"It's time to leave, Magic. We should call *Freedom* and get her headed our way while we get in a few more dives. The weather's getting worse and our exit is going to be on a fully loaded inflatable, so we need to quit while we're ahead. We can anonymously pass on the coordinates to some historic philanthropic group after we're safely out of all this and far enough removed in time and distance to keep the discovery from coming back to haunt us. Or not. This reef is spectacular just the way it is. We were careful. Those who come after us may not give a damn about this fragile environment."

"Good thinking. I'll put in a call to Mai Lee right away. Trong has already set up a code with her. I'll let him do the talking. I want to tell her about the treasure, but it will have to wait until I see her."

"Yea, we don't need to broadcast our good fortune," I concurred.

After Trong hung up the MIC, he said the rendezvous was set and *Freedom* would be in position in a couple of days. Magic had only been on the radio long enough for greetings, then Trong had taken over the conversation.

"Mai Lee didn't sound like herself," Magic worriedly noted.

"I know," agreed Trong, "but the reception was bad. She got the coordinates and she knows we had a good shoot, which means she knows we found the treasure. Maybe she's still too anxious to be excited."

It was late and we thought we might call it a day when Chien let out the distress call. He had sighted a Vietnamese patrol boat headed our way.

Magic and I grabbed a couple of weapons and quickly disappeared beneath the moon pool while Trong checked the deck for anything that might literally blow our cover. He put a pistol at the ready, hidden but accessible, and busied himself with would-be repairs for the torn hull.

When the Yabuta junk pulled alongside, Trong exchanged greetings and explained his predicament. The Vietnamese were still using these old junks for patrol boats 25 years after the war. Trong remembered them well – 36-feet long with a small cabin and machine guns mounted fore and aft. Eyes were painted on the bow to ward off demons, but the machine guns were probably more effective at that than the eyes. Out of the armed crew of four, only one lieutenant seemed intent on boarding and he brought along one of his men. He took a long look around and asked Trong a lot of questions. Staring down at the flooded fake bulkhead, he shook his head. He wanted to know how this hole could ever be repaired and Trong was ready with answers. Chien came over and joined the conversation after he saw two more patrolmen emerge from the cabin of the patrol boat. It held a crew of six, not four.

Magic and I had hoped to hear what was going on above but that wasn't possible. The patrol boat had left its diesel engine running and this roar added to the noise of a splashing ocean inside the moon pool where we waited out this nerve-racking encounter with Vietnamese authorities.

In my mind, I was back in the Mekong canals trying to avoid or ambush these patrol boats. I was just as tense and full of dread as I'd been back then. The first thing we'd hear if things went wrong would be gunfire, and by the time we could respond, it could be too late for Trong and Chien.

Trong showed the lieutenant the requested paperwork while Chien offered their guests some tea. He served the tea in what I called shipboard crap-ware – that odd and cracked assortment of cups and glasses that were used on working boats around the world.

The lieutenant seemed in no hurry. Trong worried that Chien was being so charming that the lieutenant would want to join our little band of merry men.

Magic and I were not enjoying the lieutenant's tea time. We were tired, wet and worried – men used to action who had to hide and wait.

"Well, if it all goes to hell," Magic posited, "We had a good, long run at it."

"And we died rich," I added more cheerfully than I felt.

"There is that."

"It won't undo the past but it may start to make things right."

"That's the plan," Magic confirmed.

It was almost dark when the lieutenant's men from the patrol boat yelled up that they had gotten an emergency call. The lieutenant thanked

Trong and Chien for their hospitality, discussed the possibility of seeing them again and then jumped over the side onto his boat, which took off at top speed.

Once the boat was out of sight, Trong signaled below that the emergency had passed.

I came up first, visibly relieved, and gave Trong a big pat on the back. "Good for you, Trong. You pulled it off."

"I think most of the credit goes to Chien who served tea."

Chien was smiling ear to ear. "One more cup of my tea and they'd be begging to join us. But don't worry; I didn't use the good china."

We all started to laugh, loud and hard, as we counted our good fortune. It could have gone sideways so fast. We had the treasure but we weren't in the clear. It was time to get the hell out of Dodge.

The following morning, we dove one last time for whatever we could find. The fish would miss us. They had come around and kept us company for hours at a time. Theirs was a gorgeous habitat and we'd damn well make sure that anyone we might help find the remaining treasure would do so without decimating their world.

The magic wand was busily clearing me a path through the mud when a shiny glint appeared and then vanished. I took a second look and pulled out a small gold bar shaped like a slipper and engraved with Chinese characters. "WOW!" was my only response. When Magic and I finally left the dive site, we carried 36 gold bars.

"Beyond our wildest imaginations," Magic declared as we headed topside.

"Guess we do have a few tricks left in us," I observed, grateful for a good outcome to what could have been some well-intentioned, quixotic misadventure.

All four of us gathered on deck in preparation for securing the junk and getting her underway. A piece of plywood over the moon pool kept it from leaking uncontrollably but we would not get far and would not do well in heavy seas. Darkness gave us the cover we needed to weigh anchor, hoist sails, start the engines and depart. It was time and we were ready.

The weather was unstable, but the sea was not too rough for leaky junks or Zodiacs, at least not yet. We set our course for international waters and inflated the Zodiac on deck and lashed it to the side as we slipped it in the water. We attached the engine and added the fuel tank. Next we packed the treasure – very carefully – and secured it inside the inflatable. We included water and some food for emergency use. And lastly, some of the weapons were loaded.

By midnight we were in international waters and ready to confirm final rendezvous coordinates with Mai Lee. As long as the junk was seaworthy, we didn't want to abandon it, especially not before we knew *Freedom* was nearby. We felt like we were close to the end of this operation. We were exhausted and ready for sleep, libation and celebration. We were not at all ready for Mai Lee's reference to XRAY, our emergency signal that meant something was seriously wrong -- to proceed with caution.

Our response to Mai Lee was that we were running slower than expected with an ETA of noon, a day and a half later than we would actually arrive at the coordinates.

The communication ended and we were all speechless, stunned.

Magic punched the air and spun around. This was not how things were supposed to work. Mai Lee and Benny were not to be put in danger. What had gone so wrong and how could we fix it?

Now the junk was critical. We had to keep her from taking on too much water. Any rescue would require the junk and the Zodiac and the best skills we had accumulated over a lifetime of rescues.

Chapter Twenty-Nine

When Liam called Isabella from the yacht club, she had almost forgotten how shamelessly she had flirted with him to get the information he now offered her with ever burgeoning expectations. *Freedom* was back and he was looking forward to seeing Isabella again and to taking her out. He wasn't sure when the yacht had arrived because he'd been on vacation for a while, but she was here now and he hoped Isabella was still interested in both the yacht and in getting together. Isabella expressed her gratitude and said she'd see him soon.

The next day found Mai Lee and Benny standing by, having completed the process of resupplying and refueling the boat. They knew the exploration could take awhile but they wanted to be ready for a distress or good-news call. Upon their arrival, they had let Magic know they were safely back in port.

Benny was below checking out the engine while Mai Lee loaded groceries onboard from a handcart. As she reached for the last bag, she was approached by a striking young woman she hadn't seen around the marina before.

"Beautiful yacht," Isabella said, angling to start a conversation.

"Thank you," Mai Lee replied.

"I see from the flag that she's American. We see more Australian yachts come in here, not so many from the States. She's just gorgeous."

"Glad you like her," Mai Lee responded as she kept working.

"My name is Isabella."

"Hi, Isabella, I'm sorry I can't talk more, but I've got to get these things put away."

Isabella was losing all hope of engaging Mai Lee in conversation. Even though Mai Lee was younger, she made Isabella feel like the more inexperienced and immature of the two.

"Maybe I can give you a hand with all those groceries. It'd give me a chance to see below, which would be a thrill."

"Thanks for your offer but my uncle doesn't allow any visitors onboard when he's not here."

"Where is he?" Isabella pried.

"Excuse me, but I must get back to work," Mai Lee responded flatly. She tried to appear unruffled but knew this encounter was not a chance meeting.

Isabella was becoming annoyed. She was used to getting her way.

"This isn't a very courteous way to treat someone from the U.S. Embassy."

It was at this point Benny emerged from the hatch.

"Hi, Benny, this is Isabella, who says she's from the U.S. Embassy. Did Uncle tell you that we should be expecting a visit?"

"No. Perhaps I should call Mr. Baines and see if something's wrong."

Isabella immediately recognized Baines' name. He was one of the ambassador's right-hand men.

"No, Baines didn't send me. There must be some mistake. I'd better get back to the office and clear this up. Sorry for the inconvenience." Isabella backpedaled away from the boat and retraced her steps down the dock as her entire career passed before her. Not only would she never be a field agent, she'd probably be fired if Baines got any word of her snooping. There was nothing left to do but console herself with her new best friend and all the glorious fruit drinks he could make.

Liam was delighted to see Isabella. He'd been fantasizing about her since the first day they'd met and had convinced himself that she would eventually succumb to his charm and good looks. On this particular afternoon, Isabella succumbed more to the numerous, strong concoctions that Liam presented for her consumption than any of his manly powers.

By the time Isabella had started to consider Liam for a romantic interlude, she was almost comatose. Liam helped Isabella to her car and got her to lie down. He left her with some bottled water and a barf bag, just in case. Explaining that he'd be back for her as soon as his shift ended, Liam locked Isabella in the car and took her keys. He might as well have been talking to a rag doll. As he looked down at a totally debilitated Isabella, there was just a twinge of guilt for having made her so many extra strong drinks on the house – something he hoped his boss would never know. Before rushing back into the hotel, he took one last look at his beautiful Isabella sleeping so peacefully.

Though Mai Lee and Benny had no way of knowing Isabella's current incapacitated condition, they knew she somehow meant trouble. As darkness enveloped the harbor, they raised the main and eased *Freedom* out of her slip past the horseshoe breakwater. They were running without lights, without an engine – silent and dark. Awaiting Magic's call would have to be done offshore headed south in international waters. Though Benny and Mai Lee felt fairly safe once in open seas, they still kept their firearms handy and increased their vigilance. They just wanted to hear the sound of Magic's voice. It couldn't come soon enough.

When Wu got word of the meet between Mai Lee and Embassy Girl, he had his boys split up to cover both, and he decided to join the reinforcements he sent. Mai Lee was known to his crew from her visit to Wu's shipyard. Embassy Girl had led them to Mai Lee so now all he had to do was figure out what the two women had planned and how they fit in with the American, his friend and the junk.

Though Isabella never heard the slim jim unlock her car door, she did awake in a screaming fit when two men grabbed her, pulled her out of her car, threw her into a waiting van and shoved a stinking bag over her head. She was still spewing obscenities in three languages as her feet and hands were tied. Her blinding headache and churning stomach were made all the more intolerable by the disgusting, suffocating smell that enveloped her. She was sure she was going to die -- reeking of piña coladas and dead fish. Isabella's rising panic was accompanied by loud descriptions of who she was and how much trouble her captors were in, followed by more obscenities and finally heaving. The bag now had to be removed and thrown out of the van for everyone's sake. Before she could get a look around, Isabella's head was covered in another equally disgusting sack and she was shoved hard against the side of the van. She had never felt so alone or afraid. Already disoriented by the liquor, she lost all sense of her bearings as she sat stunned, a prisoner being hauled away over a bumpy road. She realized no one would know where she was; they wouldn't even know where to start looking for her. Since it was Friday, it would be at least several days before anyone knew she was missing. With a mounting sense of terror, Isabella started a new round of screaming which was met with a hard blow across her bagged face. Wu had given strict orders she was not to be killed; he didn't say anything about roughing her up.

When the van came to a stop, it was in front of an abandoned equipment shed several miles from the yacht harbor in the middle of nowhere. Wu and two of his men met the van. Isabella was kicked out of the van at Wu's feet. He sat back in a chair that seemed to appear from nowhere. Isabella struggled to sit up and tried to remove the bag. She wasn't screaming now, just sobbing and whimpering.

When Wu pulled off the sack, Isabella, though hobbled, bolted in the opposite direction.

"We finally meet face-to-face," Wu began. "You have been interested in me for a long time. No more snooping. Just ask me what you want to know."

"You're mistaken," Isabella whispered. "I'm just a translator at the U.S. Embassy."

Wu snatched her up until her face was next to his. "Translate this: You can tell me everything now or you can tell me later, but now less painful."

Isabella didn't even know what she knew but she blurted out why she was interested in Wu and her suspicions about *Freedom's* owner and his friend.

"You should worry about them, not me. I think they're smuggling guns or something. That's all I know. Just let me go and I'll leave the country. I'm no threat to you. There's no one working with me. I never even filed one report about my suspicions concerning any of this."

"That's good to know," said Wu, releasing the girl who fell back in the dirt. She was even more expendable than he had thought. He would never be linked to her disappearance. "You live for now because you may have done me a great favor tonight."

Wu stood up, cleaned his hands with his white handkerchief and got into his car.

"Bring her in van. Keep her quiet and pretty for now."

Once again, Isabella was tossed in the van -- this time with a gag but no bag.

Wu took two calls as his black Mercedes sped through the night. One informed him that Embassy Girl's car had been hot-wired, driven back into Bangkok and parked near her apartment. The other call came from his crew at the yacht club who related that *Freedom* had pulled out of the harbor and was headed south along the coast. Her every move was being tracked on radar and Wu's boat was standing by.

If the American really was making a movie, he wasn't going to like the ending Wu had in mind.

Chapter Thirty

Mai Lee and Benny knew they were being followed. They had just gotten a call from Magic and knew that everything was a go on his end but their end was looking compromised -- first the girl and now the boat on their tail. The blip on the radar was closing in fast. As they took their positions on deck, they heard the bullhorn warning to shut down engines and prepare to be boarded by the Thai Coast Guard. It didn't make any sense; they were in international waters. They could make out some insignia on the side of the motorboat and four men in what appeared to be military uniforms. But something was wrong. They decided to keep running full bore until shots were fired across *Freedom's* bow. They couldn't outrun the pursuing craft and they didn't appear to be able to outgun it, especially if this boat was attached to the Thai Navy. Stashing weapons, Mai Lee and Benny shut down the engine and prepared to be boarded.

Upon closer inspection, even in the dark, it was more than obvious that the Coast Guard crew consisted of Wu's men. Mai Lee recognized several from the shipyard. There was a woman with them, the one who'd been so inquisitive about the yacht. She looked scared to death and was being shoved around like a prisoner, not an accomplice. Finally, when everything seemed secure, Wu pulled his hefty frame onboard. He had one of his men take

Isabella below and he sat down directly across from Benny and Mai Lee in the cockpit.

"We are your new passengers and we go where you go. We only need one of you to sail the yacht and to make contact. If one of you tries something, we kill the other. Now I'd like a whisky. Go, big sister, get me whiskey. And be quick about it. You slow, I kill your brother." Wu had done his homework.

Mai Lee searched Benny's face. He was holding up fine. She went below, grabbed a bottle of Jack Daniel's and a glass and delivered Wu his drink.

"Looks like all we have on this boat are half-breed women. What is the world coming to?" Wu remarked after watching Mai Lee pour his drink.

Wu was taunting them but he didn't get the reaction he wanted. After all, Benny and Mai Lee were no strangers to pirates and certainly not to insulting SOBs.

"What are your American friends up to?"

"They're making a movie -- an eco-documentary," Mai Lee responded calmly.

Wu put down his glass and slapped Mai Lee across the face. Benny jumped across the cockpit to defend his sister but was throttled by two of Wu's men who punched and kicked him into a corner.

"Isabella says you're running guns, though she's too stupid to really know."

"We're not running anything," Mai Lee declared defiantly as she rubbed her face.

"You must be meeting up soon. You leave dock in hurry."

"We don't have anything definite. It could be weeks or even months. The filming wasn't going well, and now with the monsoons, who knows? We just wanted to avoid more questions from the woman from the embassy since we're not Thai citizens."

This all sounded reasonable. Wu was impressed. If Mai Lee was lying, she was a damn good liar. Still, he had his own lie-detector test and he had always found it to be very reliable.

Wu had Jianjun, his second in command, put a knife to Benny's throat and he pulled Mai Lee close by her hair.

"Now, where and when are you meeting the Americans? You lie and your brother dies. I don't need him – just you."

Mai Lee didn't hesitate. "You kill him and you don't have me. You should kill us both now. We are to sail south until we're contacted. That's it. You want to know more? There is no MORE."

"Okay, tough cookie, you get boat underway. NOW!" Wu commanded angrily. "Boy, you help her but know that we watch every move."

"Jianjun, send my other boat in for now and tell Sanun to get girl ready – clean her up, make her pretty." Wu directed while he poured himself another Jack. "Looks like we in for long cruise."

Wu's boat pulled off and headed to shore while Mai Lee charted her course south. Every now and then over the following days, Jianjun, with his bald head shining in the sun, joined her in the wheelhouse to check on the heading. At times, she was told to put *Freedom* on autopilot and get below and make a meal. Mai Lee was cooking for seven now – Wu and his three men, Isabella, Benny and herself, though she wasn't hungry. She was too scared and angry to eat. She thought about drugging or poisoning the whole rotten lot but she was watched too closely to gain access to anything lethal and Benny always had to sample her cooking. Sometimes he cooked to give Mai Lee a rest, but the thugs preferred to make Mai Lee their personal servant girl. Whenever the two of them weren't working, they were tied up on deck or thrown in the forepeak, so sleep was almost impossible. There was always one of Wu's men on watch while two slept below.

After Wu had finished most of the Jack Daniel's the first night, he'd propelled his ample frame through the hatch and toward the stateroom where Isabella was being held. Sanun opened the door and slipped out past Wu, no small feat in such close quarters.

"She ready, boss," Sanun passed on the information as if Isabella were a properly cured ham.

Wu closed the door and would not be seen again for a day. Isabella's loud cries abated into pleas and whimpers in all the languages she knew. None of them could save her from Wu's ruthless rape.

He would call out when he wanted meals and libation. Otherwise, he was not disturbed.

When he finally did emerge, he called for Jianjun. "She all yours now. The others can wait till you give okay."

Wu heaved himself up through the hatch and took a seat in the cockpit across from Mai Lee whose hands were tied. Benny was at the helm and watching Wu's every move. Two of Wu's men were topside – one scouring the horizon and the other busy playing with his Colt .45. It was late and the evening hung hot and damp, but Wu's presence pierced the sultry night with a distinct chill.

With a big sigh, Wu stared at Mai Lee. "I am running out of patience and you are running out of time. If you don't hear from your American friends by tomorrow morning, we end this. I get the boat. You and your brother die. I find my junk without your help. It already paid for. I just want to know what's going on with it. I have other ways to do that."

Wu pulled out a switchblade knife, opened it and held it up menacingly next to Mai Lee's face before reaching around her and cutting the rope that bound her wrists. "You go talk to your brother. I think you have some decisions to make."

It was a long night. Benny and Mai Lee's main concern was to protect the others, to not lure them into a trap. If there was no contact by morning, they needed a way to buy a little more time.

As Mai Lee served breakfast the next morning, she was surprised to see Wu at the table. He had found a club chair that almost contained the majority of his bulk. She knew he wouldn't kill her until after he was served and probably not until after he ate, though she knew murder would not spoil his appetite.

Mai Lee was weighing her limited options when all hell broke loose in the stateroom where Isabella was being held. By now, all of Wu's crew has taken turns with Embassy Girl. She had been raped, beaten, used up and discarded. But, finally, at this moment, something in her brain had exploded and she was a raving maniac screaming gibberish at the top of her lungs. She wasn't free but she was loose, no longer a caged animal but a wild, naked creature looking for an escape. Running madly through the salon, she bolted for the hatch and flew topside where she slid across the bow and stood teetering on the brink. The beautiful, confident Isabella was nowhere in sight – only a terribly beaten, hollow-eyed wild woman who could no longer stand to be alive. Before Wu's men could threaten her or hurt her one more time, Isabella jumped into the Gulf of Thailand and quickly disappeared under the waves off the starboard side.

By the time Isabella threw herself overboard, Wu had made it topside and watched the woman in the water only long enough to make sure she didn't reappear. She was now one less thing he had to worry about.

Out of breath, Wu set down in the cockpit. "You want to join Embassy Girl?" he wearily asked Mai Lee and Benny, who along with everyone else, were on deck now.

Mai Lee knew she had to make her offer sound both plausible and likely to pay off quickly.

"I still don't know where they are, but I was told if we didn't hear something by now, we should head for Koh Wai Island, which we're on course to make in just a few hours.

"We go," said Wu. "You take the helm. We keep Benny below. If this is an ambush, he dies quick."

Mai Lee gave Benny a hug as she took the wheel. *Freedom* was making eight knots, riding a following wind through growing swells from what appeared to be an approaching storm. Mai Lee stared straight ahead, her hands tight on the stainless-steel helm. Wu was right. It was time to end this thing, at least end him. She wished him and his henchmen dead. They reminded her of all she was trying to get away from – all the evil and the ugliness. One thing she knew was that she wouldn't wind up like Isabella.

Somehow she had to let Uncle Magic know that *Freedom* was in trouble, that he'd have to be careful, and she had to do this without tipping off Wu.

When she went below for a break, the long-awaited call came in. Trong spoke first in their Vietnamese code and then Magic took the phone. Mai Lee told him she awaited his arrival at designated Point XRAY and asked for his ETA, which was noon the day after tomorrow because of slow going with the junk taking on water.

During the call, Wu had hovered over Mai Lee. He had a sickening sweet smell about him and his closeness filled her with disgust.

"Now we wait," Mai Lee announced getting as far away from Wu as possible in the tight quarters. "If you hadn't sold him a crappy boat, he'd be here sooner."

Wu seemed to find her comment amusing. "What is this XRAY?"

"It's our rendezvous point. I'll show you. We'll be closing in on it in the next hour. I'll drop anchor while it's still light. Your dinner may be a little late. And I'll need Benny for this."

As Mai Lee turned to head up the steps, Wu reached out and tripped her. She fell hard on her face and cut her chin. "You watch your tone, girl, or I'll have you for dinner."

Mai Lee pulled herself up and grabbed a nearby towel to stop the bleeding before proceeding topside to take the helm. It wasn't long before Benny joined her. He was upset that she'd been hurt.

"Benny, we have to stay focused," Mai Lee whispered. "Once we're anchored, we'll have to go below again. Somehow we must give them reasons not to tie us up. Preparing meals is our best excuse for being free. We don't want to be helpless when Magic comes. When we're in the galley, we have access to the knives and the gun we put in the freezer. We'll have to do what we can when we're needed.

Benny listened carefully to Mai Lee while he prepared for anchoring, helping his sister find the best location and ensuring that the anchor was properly set. The Genoa was already furled when Benny dropped the halyard for the main and carefully folded the sail and secured it to the boom with Mai Lee's assistance.

"I'm not a kid anymore, Mai Lee. We're not going down like before, not without a fight."

"No, this time we fight," Mai Lee confirmed resolutely.

Freedom was now at rest in another island paradise, Koh Wai -- a small jewel of ecological wonderment set in a vast, shimmering sea. Covered with lush forest and beckoning with pearlescent beaches and aqua waters, it was uninhabited and appeared untouched by the outside world. Until now, until pirates appeared offshore.

Sanun had been watching Mai Lee and Benny. He didn't understand much English or Vietnamese so he couldn't understand even the pieces of the conversation he heard.

While Mai Lee prepared the evening meal, Benny was pushed over in his usual corner in the salon. He wouldn't be tied up and stuffed in the forepeak until after he'd eaten the dinner Mai Lee brought him. After the meal, she cleaned the galley and was tied up in the salon. As usual, Wu went to bed while two of his men slept and the other kept watch.

Mai Lee believed that the ETA Magic had given her had been later than when he actually planned to arrive. She hoped so, since the situation was growing more intolerable by the moment. He knew that XRAY meant trouble. He'd come tonight, or tomorrow night, when he could get the closest without being seen. She couldn't sleep though she was exhausted. Her chin throbbed but wasn't bleeding anymore. Mai Lee was really tired of being pushed around by thugs. She wasn't even afraid for herself anymore. She was more worried about the others. She, like Benny, was prepared to go down fighting. As she struggled with the ropes that bound her wrists, she longed for her mom who had spent most of her life struggling to free herself and her family.

The sea was getting rougher under a totally black sky. In the distance, lightning flashed its jagged, pointy witch fingers. The heavy, humid atmosphere was oppressive with the threat of storms. Mai Lee thought the weather seemed as capable of violence as the two opposing forces that would soon clash in its arena.

Chapter Thirty-One

The junk was still afloat after another 60 nautical miles even as the sea crashed around her and steadily seeped inside. She had made it to the far side of Koh Wai, putting the island between the junk and *Freedom*. The anchor was set and final preparation for liberating *Freedom* was underway. It occurred to me that our mission sounded redundant, but I was not amused. We had no idea what we'd find. We didn't know if the kids were all right. In our minds, Magic and I were frantic, but in our preparation, we were all business. Surprise was our best weapon and the pitch-black night our most desirable cover. We knew the junk wouldn't show up on radar, even if Mai Lee had been forced to leave it on. We weren't expected for another day, so we hoped to catch the enemy, whoever it was, sleeping.

All of us, except for Chien, were in black and Magic was in his wetsuit. Our faces were blackened and we were carrying every weapon we had – field-stripped, oiled and loaded. Our Swift Boat tonight would be the 16-foot inflatable with its Mercury 50-hp engine that had been emptied of treasure and was now being commandeered for a rescue mission.

Chien would stay with the junk. We did leave him a handgun and a rifle. He and Trong had a private talk ending with Trong giving him a big hug. We lowered the inflatable into the water and Trong got in and took our weapons and gear as we handed them over the side to him. I jumped down and started the engine, let it idle and then secured it. Once all three of us were onboard and ready to shove off, we waved up at Chien as I shut the choke, put it in gear and idled it forward.

"Go get my friends," Chien sang over the engine. "I'll cook them best welcome-home dinner ever."

It was starting to rain and the wind picked up in erratic gusts, which would help mask our engine noise. We made our way through the rolling waves with spray covering everything. As we rounded the island, *Freedom's* lights were visible in the distance. She was anchored in a cove a couple hundred yards offshore. Through the night-vision scope, we saw one armed male on deck. There was no sign of Benny or Mai Lee. We fervently hoped that whoever had commandeered the boat had kept both of them alive as bargaining chips. Since Magic believed that any pirates taking over the ship would probably stash the kids in the forepeak, this would make his best point of entry. Once aboard, Magic planned to go through the forepeak hatch to secure Mai Lee and Benny's safety before moving aft. He didn't know how many men would be below. He was facing a lot of surprises in close quarters, but he'd done this type of rescue many times before. I could tell he was resolute and ready.

When the time was right, Magic slipped over the side, looking every bit the Navy SEAL he was. He needed time to get to the boat underwater and to get onboard so we let the wind carry us forward to the opposite side of *Freedom* in a wide looping end run. As we got closer, we shut down the engine and paddled our way in without a sound.

When we caught a quick flash from *Freedom's* waterline, we knew Magic was in position to slip aboard and we were about as damn close as we could get without the possibility of being seen.

It was at that moment that the cry of "Boat! Boat!" came from the bow. After this alarm, another man emerged from the hatch. And now there were two on deck -- both firing at our position. I gunned the engine and raced forward as Trong returned fire and appeared to wound the lookout, though he kept shooting at us. I zigzagged us closer while Trong unloaded his Ruger Mini-14 on the shooters onboard who had the advantage of a steady shooting platform and a higher vantage point. Two shots rang out from below so we knew Magic had encountered more bad guys. Rounds were hitting the water all around us as Trong brought down the bow shooter. One more to go.

The second shooter, a big bald guy, who had been firing from the cockpit, started racing forward to get a closer shot right above us when he tripped on something and came barreling overboard right into our inflatable. He was all mine. In the fall, he'd lost his rifle but was most likely still armed with something deadly. We exchanged punches in the Zodiac while Trong took the tiller and shut down the engine. When Baldy shoved me hard, I held onto his arm and we both fell overboard and proceeded to beat on each other underwater. It was obvious that he was a trained soldier and knew all the moves I knew – only he was much younger and seemed to enjoy hand-to-hand combat, something I never did. When we both came up for air, I saw him reach for his boot and pull out a knife. I grabbed at his wrist and kept the knife at arm's length, but he soon slipped out of my hold and came at me. He stabbed at my chest and got a piece of my shirt and some skin. I got my elbow into his face and kicked at his groin. It was enough to stun him for a moment. The knife fell from his hand as I got my arm around his neck and jerked hard. I could hear his spine break. It was a terrible, sickening sound – the kind of sound I had never wanted to hear again.

When I surfaced with a great gasp, I heard nothing and saw no one. Trong was not in the Zodiac. I grabbed my pistol from the boat and clamored onboard. As I came over the side, I saw Trong racing down the main hatch. I came to a screeching halt right behind him on the steps – both of us staring down at a truly unbelievable scene.

There was Wu, the hulking awfulness of him, wedged in a corner of the salon with a gun to Mai Lee's head. She was trying to get away but Wu was like the giant squid enveloping the *Nautilus*. Her hands were bound and she seemed smaller than ever compared to the huge man who held her captive. His massive frame oozed out behind Mai Lee as he kept her squarely between himself and Magic who stood unmoving -- an imposing black shadow -- on the opposite side of the cabin.

There were far too many people and guns in this tiny space. The smell of sweat, fear and gunpowder was overwhelming. One man was dead in the galley sprawled across scattered pans and crockery. Benny was peeking from a forward cabin and he looked terrified and angry. I knew he was reliving what had happened to him and his sister when pirates had destroyed their family years before.

Wu remained unflinching and unyielding holding Mai Lee in a death grip. His eyes glared with hatred and something far more sinister – a total lack of humanity.

"You move. I kill her. She nothing to me and I have nothing to lose...unless you want to make a deal."

"No deal," Magic replied coldly, knowing full well that Wu would never let Mai Lee live, that he took no prisoners.

Wu was breathing heavily. He was out of options. If he was going to die, he planned to extract one last vengeance upon this earth. When he cocked his pistol, Mai Lee spun her head away from the barrel and Magic fired. Wu got off one last shot at the same time aiming not at Mai Lee, but at Magic. Both men fell to the floor. Wu was dead, shot cleanly through the head.

Mai Lee screamed and ran to Magic. I came up behind her and cut the ropes that bound her arms before I knelt down to tend to Magic. She held his head while I took a look at the wound.

"I'll stop the bleeding. We'll get you some help," I promised as I tore off my already bloody T-shirt and pressed it to the wound, which surrounded a red fountain in his chest.

Benny huddled in close and took Magic's hand while Trong grabbed the first-aid kit. It was clear that the kit was no match for the injury, but we tried to stanch the blood and keep Magic conscious. Where were those damn medevac choppers when we needed them?

"So glad you guys are safe," Magic whispered with labored breath. "We were so worried."

"Chu Magic, we wanted to fight with you and make you proud, but you didn't need us."

"I always need you and you never fail to make me proud, both of you."

We were all hovering over Magic. I kept thinking how we'd come through worse scrapes. I wasn't at all ready to admit defeat.

"Hey, you guys, no tears. Dying from a pirate's bullet is a much better story than wasting away from Agent Orange."

"You and your damn stories! How come you didn't tell us you were sick so we could get you some help?"

"There's no more help for me, Beau. Bone-marrow transplant, maybe, if they could ever find a match for my convoluted ancestry," he sighed heavily.

"You promised not to die on me," I cursed.

"Hope you're better at promises. Please take care of these kids. They deserve more from us." He reached for my hand and I clasped it as hard as I could, hoping to hold onto him, to keep him with us while simultaneously finalizing the vow I had made.

There were no more words, no more breathing, no more Magic -- just wretched sobs piercing a now suddenly quiet night. The storm had passed over and the dawn was just beginning to lighten the horizon visible through the hatch.

I closed Magic's eyes and we all just knelt by our friend, saying good-bye in our own way, recalling our own memories, not believing that he was gone. I was the first to gather myself and got a fresh sheet and wrapped Magic. With Trong's help, we took him topside and placed him temporarily in the cockpit. Overhead, the sound of wings drew our attention. Surprisingly far from land, a magnificent owl circled *Freedom* and came to rest at the top of the mast. He looked down on us for some time, and when he flew away, a soft breeze rustled across our faces as we stood in wonder. Somehow we all sensed that Magic's spirit had flown away with the owl, that our friend had gone to a place beyond our understanding. It was strangely comforting.

It was awhile before we pulled ourselves back to the grisly task before us. We rid the ship of all the bodies, including Wu's which was a logistical nightmare, requiring all the men and a jury-rigged pulley. We kept Mai Lee out of this. She just sat next to Magic and kept him company. As the last man was thrown overboard, I thought these thugs might at last do some good in this world -- feed the fish.

After the ship was purged of bad guys, Benny joined Mai Lee and the two comforted each other while Trong and I took the inflatable back to pick up Chien. His bright face darkened when he saw ours as we tied up to the junk. Once onboard, we told him what had happened and he tried to be brave but succumbed like the rest of us.

Thankfully, there was work to do. I started the junk engine one last time as Trong pulled up the anchor. We sailed her out to deep water away from fragile coral reefs and prepared to sink her. After we struck the sails, we opened all of *Discovery's* watertight compartments. The moon pool was easy to flood but we had to break open the sea strainer for the ocean waters, normally used to cool the engine, to inundate the other compartments. With the smaller, forward watertight section, we opened the thru-hull and water poured in. As *Discovery* began to sink, we got in the Zodiac with Chien and the reloaded treasure. I sat beside the boy and Trong got the engine going and guided us away from junk *Discovery*. She had been a good ship and now she'd make a good reef for whatever marine life decided to call her home. We watched as she slipped into the ocean and finally disappeared as if she'd never existed before we dreamed her up and willed her into being and now sent her back into the depths of our own collective memory. The last I saw of her was the red flag flying from her main halyard.

We were quickly back aboard *Freedom.* Chien ran over to hug Mai Lee and Benny and they huddled together and talked in low, sad tones. Trong and I unloaded the treasure and hid it in a secret compartment I had built when I first got to the yacht club, before I had any reason to believe we'd actually find anything. It was a leap of faith, a belief in the Magic Man. And now the secret place was filled with teacups and gold and all manner of treasure. Magic's last hurrah had been a big one.

Now it was time to cleanse *Freedom* of all the ugliness that had taken place inside her over the past few days. It was a group effort. We scrubbed her from stem to stern washing away all the blood and awful smells, polishing scratches and covering bullet holes. Clean linens, fresh towels and showers all around when we were done. Once dressed in our best boat clothes, we were ready to give our friend his proper sendoff.

Asking for a few moments alone on deck, I carefully washed Magic's body, took a photo of his unexpectedly peaceful-looking and always handsome face, wrapped him in a spare Old Glory he had on-hand and then asked the others to join me. We carefully placed Magic in the white shroud Mai Lee and Benny had sewn out of an old sail with Trong adding diving weights to the precious bundle. As the sun started to set, we got *Freedom* under sail with just the main up and her Stars and Stripes at half-mast. For one last time, we gathered round Magic in the cockpit, as we had done so many times before for his stories. The ones who could say something did so, and those of us who couldn't just bid him a silent farewell. I pulled a piece of carefully folded paper from my pocket. It was the poem read at Helen's funeral that I'd kept with me ever since. I now read the same words for Magic:

God saw you getting tired
and a cure was not to be
so he put his arms around you
and whispered,
"Come to Me."

With tearful eyes we watched you
and saw you pass away
and although we love you dearly
we could not make you stay.

A golden heart stopped beating
hard working hands at rest.
God broke our hearts to prove to us
He only takes the best.

I suddenly felt as if I'd lost both my compasses -- the one battered by war and the other polished by years of constant touching. Life is kind if it provides any compass of any description. I was indeed a lucky man, even though I felt totally adrift at this moment. But I wasn't alone as I felt myself being comforted by my little band of fellow travelers.

Trong, Chien and I managed a damn smart 21-gun salute with three rifles and seven rounds. Lord knows we still had enough ammunition. As always, at military services, every shot seemed to pierce the heart. We tried to hum *Taps* but that was a blubbering disaster in some unknown and best forgotten key. It sounded so bad that we started laughing through our tears. Our sendoff was a far cry from the Arlington ceremony Magic deserved, but it seemed somehow fitting for a warrior who loved the sea, loved us and rescued so many like us by magically appearing when we needed him. He would then move on without fanfare to his next mission when the job was done.

It was time. I took note of our exact coordinates and all of us lifted Magic and eased him over the side. He slipped into the sea and much too quickly disappeared from view.

I went below and brought out a bottle of Oban single-malt scotch – a precious necessity Magic always kept onboard because he said you never knew when you might want to celebrate something. I opened the bottle and shared the precious amber potion all around. It was time for a toast to Admiral James Lewis "Magic" Black and we raised our glasses toward the piece of ocean that was this sailor's final home. I then poured what was left in the bottle over my friend's final resting place.

Chapter Thirty-Two

Even though we were all emotionally and physically exhausted, I don't think any of us got much sleep the night of Magic's sendoff. All the teacups in China and all the gold in the world wouldn't bring Magic back, but we could set a few things right, which was his last wish.

We all gathered in the salon leaving *Freedom* on autopilot. I spread charts and maps across the table and we started our decision making by pinpointing our current location off the southern coast of Vietnam. After Mai Lee recounted the story of the woman from the embassy, it was clear we couldn't return to Bangkok. The State Department would be looking for Isabella and one of her last sightings would have been at the Ocean Marina trying to get aboard *Freedom*. We would never be able to explain what had happened to Isabella or what we were doing buying a junk from a known underworld figure, or why we were hauling around a boatload of treasure.

Everyone was waiting for me to speak. They were afraid that what they had hoped for had died with Magic. They had experienced many unkept promises in the past.

"Magic's plan for the treasure was for it to be used to build new lives for all of you in America and that's still the plan," I explained. "However, he was very sketchy about how to get from here to the

States, so we're going to have to make it up as we go along."

"Like Magic did with his stories," chirped Benny.

I laughed. "Exactly right, Benny. Now the only way I can see to do this with the least amount of scrutiny is to just sail *Freedom* all the way home. It will take us several months but we can do it. When Magic brought *Freedom* over, he sailed from San Diego through Hong Kong and on to Bangkok," I pointed out on the map. "But I live on the east coast, here in North Carolina, so it appears that we should sail south to Singapore then up the west coast of Malaysia to the Bay of Bengal, around the southern tip of India, northwest to the Gulf of Aden, north through the Red Sea, out the Suez Canal to the Mediterranean, west to the North Atlantic and west home."

Everyone was watching my finger travel across the map.

"It's a good thing we all like to sail," Chien observed. "But I'm going to need more recipes."

"This is going to be a mighty undertaking, a trip halfway round the world so it will be an education in itself on every level. For Chien, Benny and Mai Lee, I think keeping a journal would be a good thing not just for you personally, but to add to your extracurricular activities for college entrance credit. Trong has agreed to keep the ship's log and I plan to take lots of photographs and videos. We will be seeing much of the Earth's beauty – a truly priceless treasure presented to us during this once-in-a-lifetime opportunity. Our journey needs to be appreciated as much as our destination is anticipated. Helen taught me that."

"So we'll all stay together and go home with you," Mai Lee summarized wistfully.

"That's the plan if it's agreeable to everyone."

"We all vote like Americans," declared Benny. "I vote YES!"

Spontaneously, we all put our right hands across the table, stacked them one on top of the other and let out one last "Hooyah" for Magic.

I charted our initial course and went topside to adjust *Freedom's* heading. A black sky greeted our new direction. How to get out of this part of the world during typhoon season was still a problem and we'd need to keep constant watch for pirates. They usually stayed close to shore and my plan was to keep us in the deep. Heading toward the equator meant that the likelihood of encountering typhoons would diminish or so I thought. In fact, the equatorial belt of calms between the two belts of trade winds was another worry. Getting caught in the doldrums with no wind was a sailor's nightmare. And though Mai Lee had refueled in Bangkok, *Freedom* was firstly a sailboat, and without wind, she'd be forced to go through a lot of precious diesel.

As usual, we were monitoring the radio's weather bands, picking up Comedy Net and Tony's Net. There had been frequent news of tropical storms but now there were reports of a threatening one forming in the South China Sea east of Singapore. Peak winds were being clocked at 50 mph and growing. The possibility of a tropical cyclone so near the equator was unheard of. As we sailed south, we'd be right in the storm's path if it was headed for the Philippines. If we kept our course near the north shore of Malaysia, we might be all right. The hope was that it would just blow itself out or bypass us to the northeast. Our options were limited. I thought of the crew I had lost in Nam and resolved not to lose this one. My resolve up against Mother Nature didn't seem very formidable so I knew it would take some good sailing and a lot of luck to keep us safe.

We had come too far to fail but we had half a world standing between us and my beloved Outer Banks. Provisions were another matter. We were low on just about everything, thanks to pirate pillaging. Our next port would be Singapore, almost 600 nautical miles away through what was shaping up to be nasty weather, which would slow us down. It was up to Chien to make what we had go as far as he could and he'd be doing a lot of fishing to augment our meager supplies if seas permitted. Luckily, the kid seemed to have a natural talent for cooking and galley management. He wanted to be chief cook-and-bottle washer and took great pride in his work. Of course, we'd all pitch in but it was good to know Chien had this responsibility handled.

When Trong relieved me on deck, we discussed the troubling weather reports and adjusted our course accordingly. He and I would have to get *Freedom* through whatever awaited her and we knew we could depend on each other. Going below, my first concern was to check on how Mai Lee was doing. She had been unusually quiet since Magic's death. I found her sitting in his favorite perch surrounded by his books and charts. Her eyes were red and she looked tired and drawn.

"Magic's death is my fault," she stammered. "I called. He came. And now he's dead, killed while saving my life."

I sat down next to her and took her hand and got her to meet my eyes. "Magic was dying. I found the doctor's report in the papers he brought with him this last trip. He had Non-Hodgkin's lymphoma, most likely caused from his exposure to Agent Orange in Vietnam. He was terminal with no more than six months to live. His only hope was a bone-marrow transplant and there was little hope of that since he was mixed race. You heard his dying words – better to go from a bullet than a painful, prolonged debilitating illness. You sensed his illness all along. You knew something was wrong."

"But I didn't try to stop him."

"There was no stopping Magic. He died doing what he wanted to do. Not everyone gets that. He probably stayed healthier and lived longer because he had this one last all-important mission. He died a hero, just like he lived."

"He didn't owe us anything. We just wanted to see him again and see if he could help us get a green card."

"Magic was best friends with your dad. He had promised to get you and your mom out, but when Saigon fell, it was total madness. He couldn't find you. He tried for years. Trong was also promised safe haven in the States for his service. Promises need to be kept. That's all Magic was doing – keeping promises."

"He promised you he wouldn't get himself killed."

"And don't think I won't bring that up the next time I see him."

Mai Lee smiled and hugged me. "We can keep them all alive in our thoughts and we can tell their stories. Magic was big on stories."

"And we can make new stories that make them proud." I was thinking as much about Helen as I was about Magic. For a moment, I wondered if Helen and Magic had found each other in the beyond and if they had as many doubts as I did about my getting things even halfway right without them.

Chapter Thirty-Three

After a couple of days of seeing a halo around the sun, building seas and steadily increasing winds, Trong and I were not at all sure that the storm we'd been monitoring was going to pass far enough northeast of us to save us from its wrath. With sustained winds of 85 mph, this storm was now officially classified as a typhoon.

We ran *Freedom* on a broad reach in the intensifying winds we were encountering. I found myself wishing for the red flag that had kept us safe onboard the junk. It had pleased the sea dragon while we had it, and now that it was gone, this dragon was definitely in a snit.

Trong and I tied off the furled Genoa, replaced the staysail with a storm jib, furled the mizzen and reefed the main to the second stay. We'd already secured the decks and broken out the life vests and harnesses. I wanted the kids in their vests and kept below. Trong and I dogged all the hatches, suited up and attached ourselves to the rails. We were in for a beating.

The skies darkened and stinging, horizontal rain pounded in with the wind, but I was thankful we might be hit with the worst during daylight hours. It would make it easier to judge the heaviest swells and avoid a broach. The barometer dropped precipitously as the winds built to 50 knots and the swells rose with larger breaks. By now, the swells were traveling much faster than the boat. We needed to rig a stern drogue, a drag to keep our speed controlled going down the face of the monster waves to prevent a pitch-pole, which would send *Freedom* end over end. Magic kept a drogue chute with a length of chain and a swivel onboard for just this type of unbelievable situation. We rigged it on a V-shaped towline from two fairleads on each side of the stern. It would ride 100-to-150 feet behind the stern and slow us down on the face of each wave like a parachute, or at least this was the plan.

Heading downwind into the walls of waves, which were now traveling at 18 knots, with gusting winds approaching 80 knots, *Freedom*'s speed, limited by the drogue to eight-to-10 knots, seemed insignificant but it gave us the maneuverability we needed. Down and up over 30-40 foot waves, never knowing if we'd be swallowed up by the seas or rise and fall to take on the next set. It was a hell of a ride. My job was to keep the boat perpendicular to each new wave. If we broached, we would roll, and that would be the end of us.

Waves roared over the stern and *Freedom's* deck was awash. The heavy seas pushed the vessel from one side to another as she struggled to overcome the water's weight and right herself. Though the fierce wind came from one direction at a time, the direction gradually changed with the cyclonic motion of the typhoon. Steering was more a wrestling match than a driving experience. We were running under bare poles, having struck the storm sail. The mainmast looked like it might snap any moment while all the lines yanked relentlessly on their cleats. It was a comfort to know *Freedom* was well-built, but storms like this had taken out better built and far bigger vessels with much more experienced sailors.

At one point, the wind calmed but the seas roared relentlessly. We were in the eye and we knew this thing was far from over. Trong stood ready to cut down anything that broke loose, that might threaten to pull us under. When the eye eventually passed over, the wind came fiercely from another direction and seemed more violent than ever. Our drogue was still on our six keeping us riding the waves without doing a 180 in the air.

I worried about the kids and hoped they were okay. I was sure they were all seasick by now. I wasn't feeling that good myself and I was on deck. They had put everything away that might fall and had surrounded themselves with cushions in the main stateroom aft.

The monster wave that I avoided was followed by its bigger, meaner brother and we rode it down at a horrific pace. We needed more than a tire drag for this one – the parachute deployed on space shuttle landings might do. I thought this was it. There was too much wind. We were going over. The chances of being rescued if we survived the destruction of the boat were minimal in this storm. No one knew where we were. No one would know we were missing. At least, there would be no worried or grieving families. We were all we had that could be called family. Trong and I exchanged one of those looks that dying comrades have shared since the beginning of time just before the boat steadied itself and came out on the other side of the wave.

Even over the roar of the wind and the seas, our laughter could be heard by the gods, the pissed-off sea dragon and anyone else foolish enough to be out in this weather.

After that macho wave, Trong and I believed we'd seen the worst this typhoon had to offer and we'd survived. Now we just had to keep doing what we were doing. Gradually, the winds abated but the seas remained heavy. With little wind, sails wouldn't be enough to give us control of this ocean. We had no choice but to run the engine and power our way through the violent swells. Though saving fuel was always a priority, getting back on course and getting through the last of this storm trumped conservation concerns. For two days, the seas remained rough and the water crashed across the deck, but eventually the swells returned to normal. Trong had relieved me at the helm when I first went to check on the kids. They were a little green and a lot scared, but mostly unbruised and greatly relieved to know we'd made it through the storm. They asked to go topside for some air but it was awhile before anyone ventured on deck without vests and harnesses. When that time came, it was amazingly peaceful and quiet, as if we'd imagined all the hullabaloo. How ironic that our treasure of teacups, which had been lost in one typhoon, was almost lost again in another, along with those who had made the incredible discovery. We certainly didn't know what else lay ahead but we'd already found treasure, beat off pirates, buried our dead and ridden out a typhoon. Next stop Singapore.

Epilogue

I felt just like one of those new world explorers when I first saw the shores of my beloved Outer Banks appear out of the dawn mist. Finally, land ho! The striped lighthouse at Cape Hatteras gave me my bearings. Vast beaches stretched out before me crowned by forests of live oaks and loblolly pines. It was still there, battered by the waves and winds and too damn much development. Sand dunes, covered in waving saw grass, beckoned me home.

All of us were out on deck with *Freedom* under full sail with our well-worn Stars and Stripes snapping in the wind. It was hard to believe our voyage was coming to an end but I sensed this was only the beginning of our adventure together. We had logged more than 10,000 nautical miles over the past six months – a trip halfway round the world that was beautifully photographed and carefully documented. We were fit and tan and full of hope – treasure hunters, pirate slayers, big-wave riders, equator-crossers and damn lucky to be alive. We had stories to fill a lifetime and enough forged-under-fire camaraderie to build a family.

Mai Lee had learned to dive and honed her sailing skills. Benny took to photography and seemed to have a good eye. Chien has amassed a recipe book that was impressive, if a tad heavy on fish dishes. All had spent time borrowing books from Magic's library, learning U.S. history, improving their English skills and boning up for their college entrance exams.

Trong and Chien had become even closer and talked of starting a business in boat charters. I wasn't at all sure I wanted to see another boat for a long time. I thought of Ulysses who grew sick of the sea and said he was going to place an oar on his shoulder and walk inland until he met someone who'd ask, "What's that?" and there he'd settle down and make his home. Though I was weary of being at sea, I wouldn't be able to live a life without oceans, without those vast unknown horizons uncluttered by man. And neither it seemed could Ulysses who had one mission after the Trojan War – to return to his island home of Ithaca where he had once been its king. I could do without the throne but I had missed my own island home and was anxious to return, not alone, but with my new family. I wanted to make them feel welcome, as welcome as Helen and I had been made to feel so long ago.

I ached from the thought that Helen would not be waiting for us, that she wouldn't be able to mother these kids or bring that sweet peace to my life. I took comfort in knowing that Helen's presence would be felt in her art, which would surround and embrace us and remind us of what matters. And Magic would still be a force in the universe – making things right, keeping promises and hopefully saving my ass upon occasion.